CW00705660

Praise for *A World of O...*

'*A World of Other People* is a powerfully imagined, elegiac homage to love, heroism and poetry ... an intimate private drama, set against the immense and tragic backdrop of European civilization tearing itself apart'   Prime Minister's Literary Awards Judges, 2014

'A fine, absorbing novel – darker than *The Lost Life* but equally eloquent and assured. Carroll's re-creation of a distant and now long-lost world is vivid and tactful'

Andrew Riemer, *The Sydney Morning Herald*

Praise for *The Time We Have Taken*

'Carroll's novel is a poised, philosophically profound exploration ... a stand-alone work that is moving and indelible in its evocation of the extraordinary in ordinary lives'

Miles Franklin Literary Award Judges, 2008

'The result is a deeply satisfying encounter with the empty spaces that the suburb failed to fill both between people and inside them. The surface of Carroll's writing is deceptively calm ... Carroll takes time to tell an untidy story with a gentle sense of wonder. His prose whispers loud'   Michael McGirr, *The Age*

'It is the creation of a larger concept of suburban life in all its transcendent possibilities that makes this novel so special. Carroll's revelations of these beautiful insights into our utterly ordinary world make him a writer worth cherishing. His prose is unfailingly assured, lyrical, poised'   Debra Adelaide, *The Australian*

Praise for *The Gift of Speed*

'Carroll's gift for evocative storytelling … had me captivated'
Australian Bookseller & Publisher

'A novel of tender and harrowing melancholy' *Le Nouvel Observateur*

'Carroll's a rare beast in that he writes with great affection and understanding about life in the suburbs … A lovely rites of passage novel that is oh so carefully crafted and captures the evanescence of time to perfection' Jason Steger, *The Age*

'Carroll's writing is astonishingly assured'
James Bradley, *Australian Book Review*

Praise for *The Art of the Engine Driver*

'Subtle, true and profoundly touching' *Le Monde*

'A veritable gem … a beautiful discovery' *Elle France*

'An exquisitely crafted journey of Australian suburban life … fresh and irresistible' Miles Franklin Literary Award Judges, 2002

'a little masterpiece' *Hessische Allgemeine*

Praise for *The Lost Life*

'Carroll's prose is limpid and assured ... [a] poised and beautifully burnished work. Carroll's control is masterly'

Andrew Riemer, *The Sydney Morning Herald*

'Carroll's ability to turn an ordinary moment into something sacred makes this novel a profound exploration of human desire, endurance, maturity and regret' *Bookseller & Publisher*

'This novel will consolidate Steven Carroll's reputation among Australia's literati ... Carroll is as much the literary ringmaster as novelist in *The Lost Life*, but remains as "rewardingly eclectic, intelligent and involving as ever"' *The Week*

'[a] brilliantly envisaged novel ... few novels begin with such measured elegance' *The Sunday Tasmanian*

'its capacity to evoke a kind of sharp, sad nostalgia for an unlived past takes you by surprise. To enter the narrative is like entering into a slightly faded but exquisitely tinted photograph encased in gilded frame' *The Canberra Times*

'this is not so much a departure as an arrival ... Carroll's fiction is distinctive for the way his clean prose decelerates experience, puts aside the urgings of linear temporality, to reveal a richness that habitually evades us ... his beautiful and poetically attentive novel retrieves a warm, beating heart from Eliot's haunted, stark, magnificent work of art' *Australian Literary Review*

'Carroll's prose has a sublime rhythmic quality ... almost as if he has sung the words on the page' *Australian Book Review*

Praise for *Forever Young*

'No Australian author has better evoked the sense of change, the ravages of time, the obligation to self as well as to others. *Forever Young* is on one level about nostalgia, without ever succumbing to it. There is pathos but no patronage in its chronicling of post-war suburban sprawl and the drift back to the inner city. You can leave the suburbs; you can even leave Australia; you can, in a word, leave home, but home will not leave you. At every turn this exquisitely crafted novel can widen our notion of what it is to be human, then, now and, possibly, later'　　　　　　*The Sydney Morning Herald*

'The title of this fine novel speaks ambivalently to a longing for lost youth, and to the desire to escape its sentimental claims'
　　　　　　　　　　　　　　　　Peter Pierce, *The Australian*

'Carroll ... transmutes the grey facts of daily life into light and luminous art'　　　　　　Geordie Williamson, *The Australian*

'Six novels that explore particular characters as they engage with a deep personal understanding of place, time, history, thought and sensation add up to a considerable achievement ... *Forever Young* shows a writer at complete ease with a style that he has developed over a considerable period of time'　　Brenda Walker, *The Monthly*

'As a psychogeographer of postwar Melbourne, Carroll is always fascinating. He has a way of embedding living stories in the fabric of the city and then binding them together'　　*The Saturday Paper*

'A very fine and significant achievement'　　*Adelaide Advertiser*

Steven Carroll was born in Melbourne. His first novel, *Remember Me, Jimmy James*, was published in 1992. This was followed by *Momoko* (1994), *The Love Song of Lucy McBride* (1998) and then *The Art of the Engine Driver* (2001), which was shortlisted for both the Miles Franklin Award in 2002 and France's Prix Femina literary award for the Best Foreign Novel in 2005, *The Gift of Speed* (2004), which was shortlisted for the Miles Franklin Award in 2005, *The Time We Have Taken* (2007), which won both the 2008 Commonwealth Writers' Prize for the South-East Asia and South Pacific Region and the Miles Franklin Award 2008, *The Lost Life* (2009), which was shortlisted for both the 2010 Barbara Jefferis Award and the ALS Gold Medal 2010, and *Spirit of Progress* (2011), which was longlisted for the 2012 Miles Franklin Award, and *A World of Other People* (2013), which was shortlisted for the South Australian Premier's Award 2014 and was co-winner of the Prime Minister's Literary Award 2014. He was a finalist for the Melbourne Prize for Literature 2015, and *Forever Young* (2015) was shortlisted for the Victorian Premier's Literary Award 2016 and the Prime Minister's Literary Award 2016.

Steven Carroll lives in Melbourne with his partner and son.

Also by Steven Carroll

Remember Me, Jimmy James

Momoko

The Love Song of Lucy McBride

The Art of the Engine Driver

The Gift of Speed

The Time We Have Taken

The Lost Life

Spirit of Progress

A World of Other People

Forever Young

STEVEN CARROLL

a new england affair

FOURTH ESTATE

Fourth Estate

An imprint of HarperCollins*Publishers*

First published in Australia in 2017
by HarperCollins*Publishers* Australia Pty Limited
ABN 36 009 913 517
harpercollins.com.au

Copyright © Steven Carroll 2017

The right of Steven Carroll to be identified as the author of this work has been asserted by him in accordance with the *Copyright Amendment (Moral Rights) Act 2000*.

This work is copyright. Apart from any use as permitted under the *Copyright Act 1968*, no part may be reproduced, copied, scanned, stored in a retrieval system, recorded, or transmitted, in any form or by any means, without the prior written permission of the publisher.

HarperCollins*Publishers*
Level 13, 201 Elizabeth Street, Sydney NSW 2000, Australia
Unit D1, 63 Apollo Drive, Rosedale, Auckland 0632, New Zealand
A 53, Sector 57, Noida, UP, India
1 London Bridge Street, London, SE1 9GF, United Kingdom
2 Bloor Street East, 20th floor, Toronto, Ontario M4W 1A8, Canada
195 Broadway, New York NY 10007, USA

ISBN: 978 1 4607 5109 1 (pbk)
ISBN: 978 1 4607 0572 8 (ebook)

Cover design by Hazel Lam, HarperCollins Design Studio
Cover images: Woman by Bettmann/Getty Images; The Dry Salvages by Philip Scalia/ Alamy Stock Photos; all other images by shutterstock.com
Typeset in Berthold Baskerville by Kirby Jones
Author photograph by Rebecca Rocks
Printed and bound in Australia by McPherson's Printing Group
The papers used by HarperCollins in the manufacture of this book are a natural, recyclable product made from wood grown in sustainable plantation forests. The fibre source and manufacturing processes meet recognised international environmental standards, and carry certification.

CONTENTS

Prologue

The rock rears up from the water like the remains of a giant whale. Surging around it in a continuous roar as they dash and withdraw, the waves make a sound all their own. Local sailors call it the *rote*: a moan, a roar, a primeval groan; it is the very voice of the rock itself, heard for miles around. In calm waters, sea birds nestle here, the granite whale enduring a white mantle of bird droppings, while seaweed, brown and green, clings to its edges. The smaller, surrounding rocks bare their teeth in the moonlight. They are a sailor's last seamark before setting out, and the first coming back in. The Dry Salvages. *Les Trois Sauvages*. Savages.

Hunching in darkness, they wait. That sound, their only give-away. When the cloud parts, the moon shines down on the whale hump and jagged teeth. Another cloud and they disappear into the haze of night. Waves come and go, light and dark do battle. On the shore, holiday houses, boats and chowder bars glow in the night; the thump of a dance band floats out over the water. The rocks are indifferent to it all.

Ships have shattered on these rocks. Crews, crates, bits of boats, rigging and torn sails floating out to sea or washing up on the beach. Ships' bells have sunk to the depths; their clocks, stopped at the moment of their sinking. But the rocks remain. Before you, and after you. Unmoved and unmoving, for all manner of fated things will come to them. Indifferent to time — the neat divisions of past, present and future are meaningless. They are a watery world unto themselves.

And as much as fishermen and sailors might use them to chart a course, the rocks don't care. People *use*; rocks abide. People come and go, leaving almost no trace; only the rocks remain, before you and after you, a primeval hump in the moonlight surrounded by jagged teeth, exhaling a continuous roar, a deep groan heard for miles around proclaiming *I am.* Now visible, now hidden, they are the beginning of a journey or the end of one.

PART ONE

A Flaw in the Crystal

1.

Unobserved by the gathering in the parlour, the long, lingering high note, swelling as it hovers, finds the weakness in a crystal glass. A tiny hole appears, a stigmata through which the red wine, drop by drop, falls onto the white tablecloth in an ever-expanding stain.

But no one sees it. Everybody is too captivated by the young woman and her voice. So too is the young woman herself. The gathering in the parlour is perfectly still. She *has* them. Notes have never poured from her so effortlessly, and even as she sings her song, she is curiously detached, as if watching from out there in the audience. She brings that long, lingering note back down to earth, a high-flying bird returning to its keeper, and begins the second verse, slowly building once again to the chorus. And all the time, she *has* them. She knows it. All eyes are on her. Especially one pair, the darkest eyes she has ever looked into. 'The wave dreams on the beach,' she sings, 'my delight is alone,' aware, more keenly as the song progresses, that the young man, her friend's cousin, is watching – the corners of his lips (and she notes the primness of his mouth) turned ever so slightly upwards in the hint of a smile. A

Gioconda smile, she thinks, momentarily distracted from her song of waves dreaming on the beach and lone delight.

Deep into the song again, she tells herself, don't look, don't look at him. But of course, she looks. It is both exciting and disquieting. Disquieting because all her life she's been told the value of measured living, of restraint. So it is both thrilling and troubling. Like indulging in some delight she knows is forbidden. All of which nearly distracts her from her song and all those dreaming waves that have suddenly become associated with that Gioconda smile. He, in front of her in the parlour, but for all the world a lone figure on the beach, listening to the siren song of the sea.

And it is as she is once again building to the chorus, the effortless notes thrilling, and made more thrilling by the close intimacy of the parlour, that she sees some of the audience turn to the table behind them. When they turn back to her their lips are moving, they are murmuring to each other, but she can't hear what they are saying.

Behind them, out of sight, the red wine, drop by drop, falls onto the white tablecloth in an ever-expanding stain. The stigmata, created by the combination of one long, high note and a weakness in the crystal from which the wine falls, drop by drop.

The last of her soaring notes comes to earth. Everything is silent and still. Then the applause breaks the spell, and those who turned from the singer to the table behind them turn once again to the object of their astonishment, informing those around them, pointing at the glass, until a small crowd gathers.

But before Emily can discover the cause of the distraction, her friend, Eleanor, whose house she is performing in, moves to the front of the parlour, claps her hands, and announces that a small reading will now take place. And that is when the young man steps forward and stands beside her.

'Miss Emily Hale,' Eleanor is announcing to the audience, 'and Mr Tom Eliot will now perform "An Afternoon with Mr Woodhouse", short scenes from Miss Austen's *Emma*.' With that she leaves them to it and Emily watches with amusement as her friend's cousin, Tom Eliot, immediately assumes the manner of Mr Woodhouse, and after briefly setting the scene and the characters coming to dine with Mr Woodhouse and his family, and after remarking on the weather and how they shouldn't be out in the cold for it is bad, very bad for one's health, that he is sure it will snow tonight and they'll all be marooned here, he begins extolling the virtues of thin gruel.

'I recommend a little gruel to you,' he announces to his guests in the manner of a middle-aged Englishman, which, Emily notes, seems to come to him quite naturally. He eyes a young woman in the audience (in a way, she suspects, that he would never dare in 'life'), and speaks directly to her. 'Before you go, if the weather lets any of us go … it will snow tonight, I know it will snow … you and I will have a nice basin of gruel,' he says, with a crisp, ironic touch, the young woman, the audience, as well as Emily, bursting into laughter. Who'd have thought, Emily thinks: so shy, so intense, but really very funny. Bit of a comedian, actually. 'My dear Emma,' he continues, turning to Emily, the comedian in him becoming more pronounced with every line, 'suppose we *all* have a little gruel. Basins of gruel for everyone. Let's not be selfish!' The delivery is pure vaudeville and there are loud groans and further laughter from the audience, and Emily, watching as he goes on to extol the wholesomeness of boiled eggs and boiled food in general, is puzzled again by the way someone who seems so shy (for she and he met briefly before the show) can be so at ease, even confident, on a stage with a script in his hand.

When he is finished his lessons on the weather, the certainty of snow, the virtues of thin gruel and the wholesomeness of boiled eggs, the audience is lit with smiling faces. He turns to his cousin, Eleanor, sitting in front of him, and cautions her on the hazards of walking out into either snow or rain. 'My dear Miss Fairfax, young ladies are delicate plants. They should take care of their health and their complexions. My dear, did you change your stockings? Young ladies are delicate plants ...'

As Eleanor nods emphatically, Tom steps back and Emily steps forward, staring at Eleanor and assuming the crass haughtiness of Mrs Elton.

'What is this I hear? Miss Fairfax going out in the rain! Going to the post office in the rain! This must not be, I assure you – you sad girl, how could you do such a thing? It is a sign I was not there to take care of you.' Emily pauses, scanning the smiling faces, satisfied with her delivery. But there is also a trace of sadness in her satisfaction, for she is more than familiar with the Mrs Eltons of this world. She lives with one. She continues. 'To the post office indeed!' and here she focuses on the same young woman to whom Tom recommended thin gruel. 'Mrs Weston,' she says, 'did you ever hear the like? You and I must positively exert our authority.'

The young woman nods firmly in agreement while the gathering applauds. And the applause no sooner dies down than a violin is heard, a short phrase that is Emily's cue. 'Music,' she says rapturously. 'Ah, music! Oh, I dote on it, dote.' She is looking at both the audience and Tom beside her. 'As I said to Mr E,' and here she gives Tom a big theatrical wink, the audience joining in on the joke, 'don't give me two carriages, don't give me enormous houses, but I could not live without music. No, life would be a blank to me.' With the word *blank*, Emily raises her eyebrows, as though fed up with the impossible silliness of her own character, the audience responding with smiles and laughter.

And so they continue, the two of them, side by side, playing out their privately rehearsed roles: nervelessly, warmed as much by the applause of gathered friends and family as by the fire. And all the time, the crystal glass measuring, drop by drop, the passing time. There they were; there they are.

* * *

Why do some nights feel as though they were always waiting to happen? Or have already happened, and will again? And why don't we know it then? Why is it only afterwards that we say, yes, *that* was when my life turned?

Emily Hale was twenty-two, with theatrical aspirations; Tom Eliot, a twenty-five-year-old philosophy student with poetic ambitions. Still children really, for all their sharp minds and clever talk. And over the next forty years, in many ways, they stayed like that. Children, sailing towards or eternally returning to this night. The house where they met, substantial but modest, with its tall, V-shaped New England roof and crisply defined white windows, has changed little over the years. If at all. There they were: the players, the place and the time. The February snow still high along the sidewalk and over the lawn, the front hedge still thick with the brown metallic leaves left over from autumn.

The front parlour itself, where their little plays were played and their songs were sung, is visible from the street where Emily is now parked. Not such a large parlour, but large enough for their games. They were close that night, all of them, the players and those who had come to be entertained. A gathering that you might call an audience, but which was, more accurately, a collection of family and friends, warmed as much by the assembled humanity as the parlour fire.

Miss Emily Hale – and she thinks of herself as a miss; even, in less charitable moments, as a spinster – is sitting at the wheel of her Ford roadster (which she has scrupulously maintained over the years), staring at the house in bright summer sunshine. The year is 1965, and much has both happened and not happened since that night in 1913.

He was just Tom Eliot then. A young philosophy student with a secret destiny. For he had, she gradually came to learn, more than just poetic ambitions — he was preparing himself for the *life* of poetry. By himself. In private. Alone. All of which he confided to Emily Hale not long after their night of amateur theatre. And she knew, even then, that what he was telling her he had never told anyone. It was his offering. His gift. His declaration, even if the word *love* was never spoken.

His confessions also told her that these ambitions he cultivated were more, much more, than just a young man's flights of fancy. For there was iron in his will. In his confidence. A confidence that was puzzling, considering his shyness — his almost unbearable shyness when in society, especially the society of young women. But not with her. For she was to learn very early on that there were at least two Toms: the public one, whose impeccable manners combined with mischievous wit to conceal his shyness; and the private one who was sure of himself well beyond his years. That was the thing, she muses, her hand resting on the satchel beside her on the front seat of the car: he was oh so sure of himself. Someone who knew exactly what he wanted to do, knew exactly the kind of writing he wanted to create and — he was happy to tell her — knew that nobody else was doing because *he* hadn't invented it yet. Oh yes, amid all the social shyness there was a core of confidence the likes of which she'd never observed in anyone before. Not one of those who look famous before they are, but one of those whose success and fame surprise and perplex nearly everybody because they never saw it coming. But she did.

He had told her, and with great excitement (such that she sometimes feels as though she too were there), about walking into the Harvard Union Library one morning and discovering a book – *The Symbolist Movement in Literature*, by Arthur Symons – that transformed his poetic ambition into a secret destiny. A morning that seemed to deliver his whole future to him on a paper-and-ink platter printed far away ... Archibald Constable & Co Ltd, London, 1899. What it must have been! The book had never been touched. Tom, the first reader. Like, she imagines, opening a long-lost document that had been waiting just for him and stumbling onto the answer to a secret code he'd been trying to crack for years. What was the day like, she wonders, and would he have noticed? Or noted the comings and goings in the library reading room? Had he been troubled by the occasional coughing or whispered conversations that come with every library? Barely. If at all. For he'd been doing more than reading, he'd been communing with the spirit of a dead poet whose life and work featured in the book: Jules Laforgue, born in Montevideo of Breton parents on August 20, 1860; who died the year before Tom was born; and who now, in his own words, resided in the well-furnished rooms of infinity. But who also, from that day, lived on in Tom, as the soul inhabits the body. He'd never heard of Jules Laforgue before that morning, but not a day would go by afterwards, she liked to think, when the magic and the secret thrill of that morning would not come back to him. There are some books that have a far greater impact than they really ought to simply by being the right book at the right time – meant for one reader only.

And when he rose, stepped out of the library and onto the street (the world suddenly lit with irony, like the verse he'd just read), did the retreating omnibus wink back; did the young woman crossing the road for the short cut into Harvard Yard volunteer her smile as no young woman had before? Or the roses incline towards him as he passed, welcoming him into the ranks of the secret society of the elect whose doors had just opened for him? Have you not observed us before, did they all say, for we have always been here? And we will always be here now: through the blooming of the lilacs, under the April sunsets and where the yellow fog prowls the night. You belong to us, and we to you. We have been here all the time. Just waiting ...

She has since read this book and read the poet whose voice and manner he put on, like a tailor-made suit. It didn't matter that she thought little of the book itself. Tom Eliot walked into that library, and the young man that she and the world would come to know as T.S. Eliot walked out. She has no doubt about that. She was *there*. She saw it. It was everything to him. Like being handed the keys to the kingdom. For with the voice of a dead poet came the right words, and with the right words, over the succeeding few years, came the poems that seemed to be there almost before he wrote them. He never said as much when he told her, but that, looking back, is how she sees it now. There are moments, when we first hear our note as if struck on a crystal glass, that hum. That give us our key-note. The note to which all the other notes yearn, and in which they resolve themselves. This was his moment, and she envied him for it. What it must have been to see the heavens part and hear the music of the spheres play for you and you alone.

And so she sits at the wheel of her Ford roadster, staring at the house where waves continue to dream and delight waits alone. She is smoking one of the five cigarettes that she allows herself each day, and when she finishes she casually throws the butt out the window. Ha! No, she doesn't. Not Miss Hale. Instead she impatiently stubs it out in the ashtray, slowly grinding the glow out of it, then slams the ashtray shut, still edgy from a night of restless, broken sleep. Beside her, on the front seat, is the satchel she brought with her, containing a bundle of papers which she secured with a ribbon not long before she left her home in Concord, a pre-Revolutionary cottage, and drove here to this quiet Cambridge street, as she does from time to time, when the mood takes her. And her first impression is the same every time – that nothing has changed and that some nights come to us complete as if having already happened, and will again. For it is a quiet cul-de-sac. There are rarely any cars parked in the street or people about, rarely any hint of the modern world. Nothing is changed. Except that the hedge is lush now, the snow of a faraway winter has long melted, and the trees are green.

She envied him even then, and the envy is still there. He had found his note. Found the very thing that, above all, he wanted to do. But it wasn't just him. She had found it too. The stage. But whereas he would pursue that something, she would never be permitted to. And as much as she envied the confidence he radiated, she envied also the freedom that made his pursuit possible. Her step-parents (her mother's mind went at an early age, and, when she was a girl, Emily was delivered over to her mother's sister) recoiled at the thought of their charge on the stage. It was not only beneath her, it was beneath them. Everybody would be diminished. Tarnished. It was impossible. You silly girl, her aunt with the voice of Mrs Elton tells her; you silly girl, the aunt who is long dead. For Emily is now seventy-four. She shakes her head. Seventy-four, when did that happen? She argued with them, she pleaded, but Uncle John and Aunt Edith prevailed. And so she made do with amateur theatricals, and teaching drama and speech and song. At first with regret, and gradually, as the years passed and whatever moment she may have had passed with them, resignation. To find your something, pursue and live it, seemed the most exquisite way to live.

At the same time, when he told her about the poems he had written in those moments of confession bestowed upon her and, she was certain, no one else – those poems upon which his whole sense of destiny was based – she was unsure. Even puzzled. Oh, he might be confident, but was his confidence misplaced, after all? For they were about strange people, with odd names like Prufrock. Who is called Prufrock? It was a name you might find in Punch and Judy, but in serious poetry? And as much as she envied his confidence, she couldn't help but wonder about his judgement. For all the seriousness of his demeanour, and for all the lofty esteem this young philosophy student was held in, there was something unstable, almost unreliable, in him. Even deeply flawed, the way those who lack judgement often are. Like the crack in Mr James' golden bowl. Or the flaw in a wine glass that renders it useless.

Through the hedge she can see the door of the house open and a woman shake a mat in the spring air. Emily Hale turns the ignition key and the car starts up, not as smoothly as the modern engines of modern automobiles, but reliably there when summoned. A solid vehicle. And she, synonymous with the car. For Emily Hale is seen, she is sure, as solid Boston through and through: no extremes, no more than five cigarettes a day, perfect speech and upright bearing. But it is a solidity that has always come with occasional outbreaks of indulgence, be it a bright floral dress that once prompted someone to observe at a garden party that Miss Hale had brought her own garden with her. Or speed. However much she may value decorum or embody restraint, she knows of nothing that stirs her quite like the blast of air on her face when the window of the car is down, and the rush of laneways as they rise up to meet her and fly by. Nothing like letting that touch of recklessness into a life defined by propriety to clear the head. And so as she pulls out from the kerb, it is with a sudden screech of burning rubber that lifts the head of the woman in the doorway, absorbed until then on shaking the dust from her mat. Miss Hale, in short, has a lead foot. Luckily for her, the car is old and indulges her impulse with a response consistent with a more leisurely age, when speed was still only being invented.

The midsummer morning, although bright, is heavy and humid. Clouds are gathering. She pulls out into one of the main thoroughfares of Cambridge and steers the roadster north-east towards the fishing town of Gloucester, no more than an hour's drive away. It is a good day for a drive, so long as the weather holds.

She glances down at the satchel beside her. It is not properly closed and she can see, poking out, a yellowed envelope from old times. The English stamp bearing the face of a king long gone – a small, deep-blue stamp that you would only find now in somebody's collection. Old papers from old times. Old stamps. And dead kings.

As she leaves the city the clouds continue to gather, and she hears the first rumble of what might be a storm. And out towards the coast she can see an elongated dark cloud, like a beast in the jungle, crouching and ready to spring.

He was Tom Eliot, the young philosophy student of whom so much was expected. She was Emily Hale, the Boston beauty with a voice that thrilled fire-lit parlours with tales of dreaming waves and lone delight. They were destined for each other.

Even created for each other. And their union, like the night that brought them together, even then gave every impression of already having happened. But it never did. And why is that? It is the great puzzle upon which she dwells every day. And every day has a question mark hanging over it.

2.

The beast in the jungle sits on the horizon, waiting, ready to pounce. There is an occasional rumble, as if coming from the beast itself. A hint of things to come, or not to come. The lead foot of Emily Hale steps on the accelerator, speeding into the past.

They went to concerts, exhibitions and recitals. In the language of this modern world, they dated, the way the young people in the town date – such as Grace, the young New York woman she tutors who has a voice that reminds Emily of the voice she too once had. But instead of meeting in diners and cafés and bars, a jukebox never far away, they met in parlours and gardens. And nearly always the same parlour and the same garden. At Tom's cousin's. The words exchanged, often as not, carefully chosen and precise, hinting at so much more. The strong emotions, and the passions that stirred them, rarely breaking the surface. Two people always on the brink of saying what they thought. And what they felt. She thinks of them, Tom and Emily, as 'they'. But this twenty-two-year-old Emily she remembers is definitely her, not someone else. And the twenty-five-year-old Tom, him. Us. And we. But 'they', all the same.

Like distant figures with whom one is intimately associated. And dissatisfied with. Even embarrassed by. There they were; there they are. Them and not them. 'They'. Characters from a novel, playing out their roles and reciting their assigned lines without realising it. As if invented by Mr James. The two of them creations of an invisible author, the very existence of whom is kept from them. Tom and Emily, Emily and Tom, always circling round the thing he would have her say, or she would have him say. Both of them too refined to say it. Implying the thing, rather, through looks and confidences. There they are, in some lost pocket of time, forever going over the same conversation, or variations of it; the conversation different with every remembered re-enactment. Players, Emily giving them a gesture here and a pose there, depending on the day and on her mood.

She remembers them, especially, on one particular afternoon, memorable because it was one of those occasions when passion did break through the surface of decorum, and emotions, if not made clear, were given air.

They are making small talk: the weather, the spring, the profusion of spring flowers, scents and smells – all charged with a peculiar urgency. What *is* that flower? Why *does* that scent distract me so? *Who* did you say has just come back from Paris with next year's fashions which she's placed in a drawer until then? The garden is a hothouse of lush vegetation. Desire and expectation are hanging in the air with all the spring smells.

And then he suddenly asks, 'Is it possible, do you think, to be in the midst of some great event, possibly the great event of your life, and miss it? Just not see it?'

'At the time?'

'Yes.'

'And only see it afterwards?'

'But miss it while it's happening. Something so natural you don't notice it, because it doesn't stand out.'

They are in the garden not long before he is leaving to go to Oxford for a year. It is a garden he's known all his life and feels perfectly comfortable in. More than comfortable, happy. A garden filled with happy memories: spring flowers, purple, red and yellow, all around, as vivid in recollection now to Emily as the green countryside gliding by outside the car window. Above her the sky rumbles again.

'While we're running madly after one thing or another, do we miss the real event?'

It is, it seems to her, put like a proposition in a philosophy class. An invitation to open up a discussion. A detached, even impersonal one, but there is unease in the way the question is posed. Urgency in the way the words almost tumble from him, as he fingers his shirt collar, looking from Emily to this vegetable world around him, and back at Emily. And there is a certain anticipation also in his words. The suggestion, in his manner, that something far more than a good discussion is resting on her response.

They are sitting on cane chairs, a jug of something or other on the table. She didn't notice what they drank that day, if they did at all; it doesn't matter. He's known the house and the garden all his life and should be perfectly comfortable and happy in it, but he isn't. He is restless, even fidgety. There is something he wants to say. But he's being vague about it. His question is couched in general, impersonal terms, but it's particular. And quite personal. Posed between two people who sense that something is going on between them, although they've never told each other as much; two young people who, and all their friends agree, have a bond – but what precisely is this bond and where is it leading? And it is one of those moments when she finds herself on the brink of saying just what she thinks, instead of circling round this event he is being so vague about. Which great event? What on earth is he talking about? Something that hasn't yet happened, or already has? Concerning him alone, or them? Is it some sort of game? The tone of the question suggests as much. He is vague; she is impatient – with him, with the day, with the world. And the garden, the garden seems to be growing, swelling into profusion as they watch.

'I think I would know. If some great event came along, I think I should.'

'Would you?'

The question is asked with a faint touch of hope. Nervous hope. He's fidgety still.

'At least, I assume so. Wouldn't you?'

'That's what I'm asking.'

'Well, I would. Anybody would.'

'You sound sure of yourself.'

In fact, she is anything but sure because she can't be certain just what he means. 'Well, as sure as I can be.'

'And is there such an event in your life?'

'A great event? Is there a great event in my life? Why do you ask? Just what are you talking about? You're an odd one today, Tom. Very odd.'

Someone once said of Emily, a comment reported back to her, that beneath the New England beauty there was a bit of a sergeant major. And they might say that of her now, but she's just giving certain feelings air. In doing that, though, setting free irritations and annoyances, she is breaking the rules about what a young woman must and mustn't do – and for that do they call you a sergeant major? The faint touch of hope drains from his face. She pauses, and because neither of them is speaking and because she dislikes such silences and is always the first one to break them, she asks abruptly, 'When do you leave?'

He looks at her, distracted by his thoughts, as if still dwelling on what they *were* talking about. 'Soon.'

'I know that, Tom. When?'

He names a date. 'That *is* soon.'

There is a sudden tender regret in the way she says this, and they both fall silent. *Soon.* And for a moment she doesn't feel young any more. Not really. As though a sudden shadow has fallen over her. And a worrying urgency comes over her as well, the feeling that if she's not careful, all things will happen soon. And the feeling lingers through their afternoon together. You are twenty-two, Emily, twenty-two. Blink and you'll be … No, don't blink.

He pulls a packet of cigarettes from his coat pocket. French cigarettes, she notices. And the moment he lights one, the smell, somehow disquieting, even distasteful, of a foreign country (one that her aunt and uncle would find morally questionable, even offensive) enters the garden and mingles with the scent of fresh spring flowers, turning it stale upon contact. Evil Europe. And the moment she thinks this she rebukes herself for assuming the attitudes of her aunt and uncle, with whom she has fought all her life for one freedom or another. All the same, these French things of his do stink.

He exhales, and there is something annoyingly affected about the whole pose. As though it's all part of some deliberated self-invention, as though he is creating himself. Or an image of some self he'd like to be, an alter ego brought back from France, modelled on those French poets he reads all the time and tells her about, who, no doubt, exhale their cigarette smoke in just such a way, a sign of their impatience with this trivial little madcap world they have inherited and have no choice but to live in, but which, all the same, they're well above. This little madcap world that barely knows what it does, but *they* do because they're so clever. Yes, he's clever this Tom, intelligent too, but not so clever or so intelligent as to resist transparent poses. Older than her, but, she thinks at this moment, so much younger. And quite possibly always will be. All of which, combined with the vague sense of being in one of his philosophy classes, brings back this feeling of annoyance. With him. With everything.

'So soon, indeed. That must be exciting. I envy you.'

Now he is surprised, no longer distracted or tense. 'For what?'

And it is here, with this simple, and, it seemed to her then as now, astonishingly uncomprehending question, that annoyance and strong emotion break through the veneer of decorum, and the frustrated passion of a lifetime's thwarted dreams erupts from her.

'For what! Your *life*. That's what.'

'*My* life?'

'You're barely back here and you're off again. You come, you go. You are free. You do as you please. Yes, your life!'

Her face is flushed, but wistful all the same, looking out over the garden as if all this spring show around her, its bounteousness and promise of full blooming, were for the benefit of others, not the likes of her.

'Don't you see? You are free to go to university. I shall never go. You are free to drift alone through foreign cities at midnight and interrogate the street lamps. To take to the stage should you desire ...'

'Heaven forbid.'

'But you are free to pursue your dreams. You know what I mean. I don't control my life. I don't, Tom, only part of it. I walk from this part of the deck to that part. That much I control, but the ship … the ship …' She pauses, frowning. 'And it's not anger I feel. Don't think that. Or resentment. I'm happy for you. Do you believe me?'

And here she places her hand on his, clasping it, she knows, in a way that daringly hints at the affections underlying the act. At the passions, yes, we had them too, she nods to herself at the wheel. What is more, she clasps his hand with the feeling that she has every right to. And having made her point, she retracts her hand and sighs. 'No, it's not anger. It's … incomprehension. That things *are* as they are, and not otherwise. When I could be you, and you me.'

She wriggles in her chair, twists about in it, almost as though she is about to spring from it. She argued that morning with her aunt and uncle (if argued isn't too strong a word) about her own ambitions. The theatre. It is her passion and she has been told often enough by her friends that with her beauty, her voice and her natural, theatrical ease, she was born for the theatre. But her aunt and uncle are immoveable. Going on the stage, they call it. With a knowing look that says only certain women go on the stage. A look especially evident in her aunt's eyes, her aunt who knows what is best for Emily (and this will not change in the coming years), more than Emily does. And so is that it? Does he simply annoy her on this afternoon (his French cigarettes fouling the garden) because the world annoys her? Because, at this particular moment, he is not her Tom but part of that uncomprehending, annoying world? And does everything follow from there?

'You're unhappy?' he asks.

'Not exactly.'

'But not exactly happy?'

'I could be.'

He pounces on this. 'Is there something I can do?'

She turns from the garden, from thoughts of her aunt and uncle and the whole annoying world, and looks at him: his hair impeccably parted, the portable Dante in his coat pocket, ash falling from his cigarette, and she is tempted to say that he could stop smoking that thing for a start. 'Not unless you can change the world.' Here she smiles, but it is a sad smile. 'Can you do that for me? Is that so much to ask? Such a little thing.' She leans towards him, indicating with thumb and forefinger the dimensions of this tiny thing she asks. There is a conspiratorial playfulness to it all that brings out an open smile of delight in his eyes, and she loves that smile. And in that moment is sure that she loves Tom too. And equally as sure that he sees this. And that he loves her. Oh yes, she's sure of all that. She *had* him.

He puts his cigarette out, as if heeding her unspoken directive, and the last of the smoke trails up into the air and out across the garden.

'Shall I banish your aunt, for a start? I've found some nice little deserted islands along the coast in my boat. Just made for her.'

'She means well.'

'Heaven preserve us from the well-meaning.'

A smile is on her face and he is as entranced by it as he was by her singing that previous year, all of which she saw as clearly then as she does now at the wheel of her roadster.

'You need a companion,' he says. 'Everybody needs a companion.'

'Companion?' And she asks this in a manner of saying, but that's not much. Not so much at all. I asked you to change the world. 'You *are* my companion.'

'A special friend, then. And more.' Here he inclines towards her, eyes her inquiringly, wondering, possibly, how far to go. Is she telling him to go further? She barely knows herself. Suddenly, words seem to flood from him. 'Much more, if you wish. Close friends! You can tell me things. Everything. And I you. We can tell each other things. The things that matter, and that you can't tell to just anyone. Only a close, a special friend. Although there are times, often enough, when I'm sure you know all my thoughts without need of being told. Know me better than I know myself. You're keen. You miss nothing. Am I imagining this? Just say, *am* I?'

The torrent ends abruptly, the question hanging in the scented air. He pauses, lingering on the hyacinths, wondering, possibly, if he has gone too far, the tobacco gone to his head like some opiate. Said too much. All the same, hinting that he is not yet finished, his lips pursed, ready to continue, the scent of the hyacinths mingling with the faint, stale smell of a French café that his cigarette has brought into the garden.

'I always feel awkward, being the first to speak up and talking like this … talking to most women.' She's watching him, and feels his awkwardness. It is impossible not to. Poor men. Poor, poor men, always called upon to make the first moves. And risk becoming fools. Becoming ridiculous. Poor men. Poor Tom. If only she could say it for him, whatever it is that he's trying to say. 'But not you. Well, not *as* awkward.'

Oh, yes, she quietly acknowledges to herself, she *has* him. But when will he say it? The garden is still and silent.

'And why is that?' she asks, poised, even flattered, but fishing for compliments, all the same.

He speaks like a man closing his eyes and leaping from a high board into a pool below. A leap of faith. 'Because, Emily, you're … you're not most women. You must know you're not. Just look at you. Of course, you can't do that. But if you could,' and he pauses, the longing clearly written in his eyes, 'you would see yourself as I do. You are extraordinary.'

There it was, plain as that spring day. A confession. For if that wasn't a confession, what is? His gaze resting on her, his words falling through the air in a slow, protracted dive: you are not most women. Just look at you … You are extraordinary. And she knew that all he was waiting for, all he required, was a word. A confirmation from her. But was she too annoyed with the world that day to give him this, and did everything flow from there? Is that it? Can our entire lives turn like that? Annoyance with the world becomes annoyance with whoever is sitting opposite you or whoever you are with?

In this case, Tom, whom she probably loved even then (the probably becoming a certainty as the years passed), and who required only a sign that his feelings were returned. How many times has she remembered this scene, and reshaped it, not saying what she is about to say and giving him, after all, that confirmation that he sought: that his feelings for her were returned.

'But you're going abroad soon. And it is easy to say these things when you're leaving. And what sort of companion, what sort of close friend, is that? More absent than present.'

'I must go away. You know that. It's all arranged. And I don't particularly relish the thought of Oxford at all. More university! But I will only be gone for a year. Is that so long?'

She leans forward, almost as though talking to a child who hasn't understood anything she has said.

'Are you asking me to wait?'

'Well –'

Before he can finish she jumps in. 'Tom, I'm twenty-two. I'm tired of waiting for one thing or another. I seem to have spent my life waiting for one thing or another. Waiting for someone to say yes. Yes, Emily, yes. But all I ever hear is no, Emily, no. Silly girl. So I wait.' She pauses, as if suddenly granted a preview, and a very plausible one, of how her life will unfold. 'Perhaps that's my lot. To wait.'

She leans back in her chair, the annoyance passing for the moment, and smiles at him. 'You say a year, but these things change. It's another world over there. Heaven knows whom you'll meet. All sorts of wonderful creatures, no doubt. Who knows what can happen.' She stops a moment, thoughtful, even a little frightened, for what she is saying is true. Heaven knows whom he will meet. And will there, inevitably, come a day when she will receive a letter, saying Emily, dear Emily ... forgive me, I am no longer what I was, I am a different Tom, the world looks different, *everything* is different here: a way of saying, 'I have met someone ...', without saying as much. All of which leaves her thinking of letters, not unlike the letters in her satchel beside her on the front seat of the car. 'But you'll write to me?'

'Write? Of course. Was there ever any doubt?' he says, almost desperate.

'That would be nice.' She knows the *nice* will wound him and for some reason she still wants to wound him ... for his uncomprehending questions, for his going abroad so soon, for the lingering stink of his cigarette — all of this and none of this — even while acknowledging that she probably loves him. And so she sways from annoyance to love, and love to annoyance. A bad day to receive confessions of love. If she understands him properly, that is. And what she has heard *is* a confession. 'And this great event of yours, perhaps we can watch for it together.'

But he doesn't hear the latter part of her offering, only the former. 'Nice?'

She sighs. 'What am I saying? More than that, dear Tom. Much more.'

He lingers on her and he pauses for a moment, while, simultaneous to his pausing, Emily grips the wheel of the car and registers a slight bump in the road. 'Tell me,' she hears him say, the words floating up through the years, 'that a year is not so long. Not really. We will be apart ...' She nods and smiles for a moment, both at the wheel and in that garden. '... but not apart. Close, without need of being in the same room. No need of letters at all. We'll simply transmit our thoughts ...' He smiles. 'Yes. Like those ...'

'Like what?' She is keen, expectant. Urging him on.

'Like ...' He looks around at the flowers and up to the sky, eyes concentrated, hand on the portable Dante in his pocket, lips pursed to speak, and as much as he has already said more than he imagined he would or could, he seems now on the brink of some fantastic confession, and Emily felt then and feels now the air trembling as he draws breath.

'Like ...'

But it is beyond him. He sighs. The fantastic thing that trembled on the brink of being spoken withdraws. Like what? Was he about to say, like those lovers who transmit their thoughts to each other without need of speaking? Like those doomed lovers whose every moment together consumes them? The Dante and Beatrice that he keeps in his coat pocket? Tristan and Isolde? And all the others? Unrequited. Divided by heaven knows what. By the annoying worlds of other ages? But he doesn't say it.

It is beyond him. And her. It is beyond the both of them. Why? Because these two people, with whom she feels intimately associated – adults, but by modern standards still children in regard to the ways of the world (and who now annoy and frustrate her, as she turns the wheel, following a curve in the road leading to Gloucester) – these two people have their assigned lines. Is that it? Like characters from a novel. A novel about the social mores and manners of a society long gone. Their lines written, their fate ordained. Creations, and yet, at the same time, the very *living* models from which Mr James could have created his characters, because they *are* that society and time, their assigned lines coming naturally to them. Added to this, are they not imitating their elders too, playing roles, even if they don't know it? As they do in amateur theatricals, their parts drilled into them to the point that they don't know they're doing it any more, and everything they say has not so much been scripted by Mr James or any such unseen author, but by the time and the place that made them: their manners and speech those of the upright and proper elders who went before. But who still keep a watchful eye on them, both in fact (her aunt and uncle) and in spirit, the framed photographs on parlour mantelpieces: ever-present elders, dead and living guardians of the script, as much as guardians of the faith.

At the age they were then in that Boston garden, she muses, the outskirts of Gloucester coming into view, we imagine there is time for things done to be undone and things not done to be done. And the awful finality of never seeing someone again is unimaginable. So it was with Tom and Emily. Time on their side, they resolve to write, like close friends on the crest of becoming so much more; that last sentence, in which he might have said the thing he wanted to say, left unsaid. Oh, she knew in her bones then, and knows now, that he came in quest of so much more. Confirmation that his feelings were returned. The indication that yes, she would wait. Of course she would. Silly Tom, was there ever any doubt? That was all she had to say, all she had to give him. But the world annoyed her that day, and the chance never came again. For at this point, his cousin, her dear friend Eleanor, comes bursting into the garden with news of someone's improbable engagement, and what they might have gone on to say remains suspended in the air along with that last unfinished sentence.

And so the three of them sit at the table, chatting of this improbable engagement, and Tom talks lightly about the intricacies of college friendships when chat about the engagement has exhausted itself.

A roguish smile lights his eyes. He goes on to say that somebody, who can't be named and can only be called 'A', hates somebody, who likewise cannot be named and will be called 'B'. 'A' recounts some casual comment of his about 'D'. 'D' hates Tom, who shall be called 'E'. 'B' and 'D' are good friends and both get in a dreadful state. 'A' is happy.

Oh, and 'C', he forgets, 'C' is suspicious of them all and just doesn't know what to think.

Grins all round. He is no sooner finished than he starts on a detailed description of the ten-reel cinema drama he is mentally writing, the title of which, he informs them with deadpan seriousness, is *Effie the Waif.* He lays the scene in Medicine Bow, Wyoming. Of course. Then, amid smiles and laughter, expounds upon the main players: Effie, the motherless little brat; Spike Cassidy, the reformed gambler; and Seedy Sam, the blackmailer. All to be staged, he assures them, at vast expense in the mountains of Wyoming. What he doesn't tell them about is the series of poems – King Bolo and his Big Black Kween – which he writes purely for the amusement of his college associates, and will continue to write in later life in London for his work associates, all prominent men of letters or in the business of publishing those same lettered men, but all, like Tom, with a part of them that never grew up. No, he doesn't let them in on this, for this is another Tom altogether. But Emily heard about these verses of his, all the same. How? She can't remember. But she did. How many Toms were there? A Tom within a Tom within … And did anybody ever get to glimpse the real Tom? Did *she*? Or was it just layers all the way through? And are the rest of us any different? Chatter, and it is chatter, about Effie the motherless brat, goes on, each of them, in turn, enlarging upon the slapstick with slapstick of their own. And so, effortlessly, the afternoon begins to slip away.

Before it does, as the light mellows, Eleanor leans forward: serious face, playful eyes. 'So tell me, Mr Eliot, how are you enjoying your visit to America?'

Tom smiles, he knows the game. 'My visit? Why, I'm St Louis born and bred, ma'am. In bricks.'

'St Louis?' Emily adds, joining in. 'And there I was thinking you were English.'

'I'm a Missouri man, Miss Hale. And we know a thing or two.'

'What do you know, Mr Eliot? If we may be apprised of the matter?'

'I must say you Boston ladies talk real fine. Yes, *real* fine.'

'And what do you know?'

'Business, Miss Hale. Flows through us like the Mississippi. And I wouldn't be speakin' anythin' less than the gospel truth if I didn't say that the government oughta just leave business alone.'

'That's very political, Mr Eliot.'

'What would you suggest we talk about, Miss Hinkley?'

A bird suddenly calls from a tree in the garden. They all look up.

'Well, I just love ornithology,' Eleanor answers, looking back at Tom.

He shakes his head. 'Not much call for that in Missouri.'

'Oh? You don't have birds in Missouri?'

'We have birds, Miss Hinkley, we just don't have ornithology.'

They fall back in their chairs, spent for the moment; the bird continues calling. Tom is relaxed with his cousin. They have been talking like this all their lives. The switch from awkward, unfinished sentences to easy, amusing, clever chat is dramatic. Like, Emily imagines, a practised actor switching from one role to another. Playing roles, trying them out. And it is at this point that she wonders if he has just been playing with her. Arranging her: standing her on a garden stair, like Effie the motherless brat or some fugitive lover flinging flowers to the ground. Playing some intricate game, the true nature of which only he knows. Or thinks he does. And in that same moment – after all his talk of his trips to Paris and London and Germany, of poetry and poems, risk and exploring life the way he explores the Gloucester coast every summer – in that same moment she can't help but think there is something not quite *there* – something ungrounded in Tom Eliot. Something not quite grown up. Leaving him prey to some act of impulsive daring one day that he might well regret. A hairline crack in a golden bowl; a weakness in the crystal. And is that also why she held back, not just because the world annoyed her?

Perhaps, she may have thought, a year might not be such a bad thing, after all.

Who knows what she was thinking. But did he take that as a rejection? For it was a proposal of sorts, wasn't it? Said the only way he could say it. The only way *they* could say it.

And when he finally rose and left the table, did he walk away convinced that he had professed his love (which she had clearly seen in his eyes that night of amateur theatricals, of dreaming waves and lone delight), only to leave rejected? Or, at best, disappointed? The world annoyed her that day:

a hairline crack preoccupied her; the time wasn't right. Who knows what she was thinking. Sentences were left hanging in the vegetable air, and they were never completed because the chance never came again.

3.

Grace is old for her age. Possibly too old. She can't be any more than eighteen or nineteen, but she seems to know too much. More, Emily tells herself as she approaches the port of Gloucester, than she ever did at her age or even later. But perhaps that's not right. Perhaps they simply knew and know different things. And perhaps, to Emily's aunt and uncle, she gave the impression of being old for her age too. Heaven knows, she never felt it.

Concord, she smiles to herself, may have a big history, but it's a small town. And Grace, new to the town, heard about Miss Hale. Everybody new heard about Miss Hale: who taught drama with a dramatic flair that was a performance in itself. And who long ago had a 'thing' with someone famous. Oh, she nods to herself at the wheel, the town got to know Miss Hale very quickly, all right. And so did Grace. And having ambitions to either act or sing or both (or perhaps just to pass the time), she came to Miss Hale, who took her in. So once a week Grace comes to Emily's cottage and Emily teaches her. They come from different ages, indeed different worlds, but she sees something of herself in this young woman, except that Grace doesn't have anybody telling her that acting is beneath her.

The confidence she radiates, Emily is convinced, is more than just that of an assertive young woman; it is the confidence of the age itself shining through her: a young age, and although all ages begin young, this one, she thinks, is particularly young. Not only will no one tell Grace what she can and can't do, the young woman radiates the kind of confidence that assumes all things are possible. How does she say it? *Do*-able. Acting is her 'thing', and she will do her thing.

Emily shakes her head as she passes the railway station and enters the final part of her drive down to the harbour. But as much as she might shake her head at any generation that substitutes the word *thing* for a real word, she feels a certain connection with Grace. A degree of affection: an affection that has grown over the last few months. She even worries about her. Not like a mother would. No, more like an older sister or a stepsister from a previous marriage, her worries a mixture of concern, envy and annoyance. Perhaps even alarm.

The previous day they did Shakespeare. *Romeo and Juliet.* Grace was reciting her lines. *Her* way. Not the way Emily would have. Not the way anybody from Emily's age would have. No affected, theatrical voice. Just Grace's voice, a New York voice. A New York Juliet. And as much as the performance was riddled with strangled vowels, Emily had to admit that the girl had something. That somehow it all worked. But slowly, something else started to concern her. For as she walked around Grace, making comments now and then as she recited her lines, she noticed a mark on the young woman's shoulder. The day was warm, and Grace was wearing a loose top that occasionally fell from her shoulder, exposing the mark. And the more Emily circled her, the more she was drawn to it. Became fixated, even. To the point that she wasn't really listening any more. And as much as she felt she ought not say anything, when Grace had finished she suddenly found herself asking, 'What have you done to yourself?'

Grace looked up from her text. 'What do you mean?'

'*That*,' Emily said, pointing at the mark with a small ruler that she carried as much for her own sense of security as to occasionally tap out a rhythm.

'Oh, that,' Grace said, pulling up her top so that it covered the mark, flicking back her bright blonde hair as she did. 'That was my boyfriend.' She paused. 'A sort of boyfriend.' And here she leaned forward, blue eyes as bright as her hair, and grinned. 'He's a bit of an animal.'

Emily may have been betrayed by a slight tremor in the hand that held the ruler. May even have flinched. As though she, Emily, had let a bit of an animal into her house. For the little animal was giggling. And was she just laughing, or laughing *at* Emily? She wasn't sure. Had she flinched? She may have. And was it a visible flinch and was that why Grace was laughing? It was possible, for the shock of the comment was what she could only call electric. And it was while Grace's giggling was dying down that Emily became once more mindful of the differences between them: too large, encompassing too many years to simply be the differences between an older and a younger sister. No, she told herself then and now tells herself again, Grace is old for her age in a way that she never was.

Grace looked up at Emily, smiling. 'It's a love bite.'

Of course. She'd heard of the term, in the same way that she was familiar with terms such as *do-able* and *thing*, but for some reason she hadn't, just then, connected it with the mark on Grace's shoulder. Silly. And part of her still feels a little unworldly, to a degree that makes the young woman worldly by comparison. And Emily a sheltered old fuddy-duddy. At least Emily thinks so. And it feels like a failure of some kind. That she is a teacher and ought to know things beyond speech and projection. And while she is contemplating all of this, she recalls Grace suddenly asking her with astonishing innocence: 'Haven't you ever had one?'

'A what?'

'A love bite.'

Grace may as well have asked her if she preferred Budweiser or Miller's. And for the second time in a matter of minutes, Emily was asking herself if she'd flinched. But this time, she felt sure, she'd held firm. 'Sounds positively vampiric,' she responded.

Grace broke into a grin again, and turned, looking out the cottage window as she spoke. 'Oh, it *is*.' Turning back from the window, as she looked down at the text, she added, 'You can bet Romeo gave Juliet one.' She paused. 'And Juliet, Romeo.'

Have you never had one? And it is again not so much the directness of the question as the innocence of it. Or is it the assumption underlying it? That, surely, everybody bears such a mark at some stage in their life. Emily sighs at the wheel. How to explain it? How, if she ever tried (and she won't), could she explain it? For it would almost be like speaking to a creature from another planet, not just another time. Our days were governed by different manners and expectations, she would begin, and what we said and didn't say (and we would *never* have spoken of such things) was determined by those manners. We lived by codes, and whole orders of feeling, that are perhaps now extinct. You have your love bites, and heaven knows what else, but will you ever be granted a touch of the sublime by a simple, yet daring, kiss on the cheek at the end of an evening, as she had after the opera one evening with Tom, and will you lie awake for hours afterwards with the sensation, the feel of a parting kiss, *still* there on your cheek – as lasting, even more so, than any love bite?

At some point a look, almost of pity, came into Grace's eyes. And Emily was on the verge of saying, there's no need for that. But of course, Emily is of an age and a place and a social circle that thought far more than it ever said, and so she said nothing.

The lesson finished, Grace paid her in cash, and Emily, as she always did, went straight to a small study, just off the lounge room. What she didn't notice was that while Grace was facing the front door, idly thinking about how to fill the rest of the day, a trick of the mirror on the lounge-room wall gave her a clear view of Miss Hale in her study. She didn't mean to look, but could not help but see Miss Hale slip the notes into the drawer of her desk. Grace took it in, then promptly forgot about it.

Emily returned, glancing at the portraits on the sideboard: of family, of friends, and a treasured framed snap of Tom that she had taken just after the Second World War on a visit to Wood's Hole — and straight away the image conjured up that whole world of vanished feelings. Did we really, did we really *feel* differently? Still conscious of the mark on Grace's neck as she approached the front door to farewell the girl — the front door that opened onto a small green that ended with Emily's church, which had been there since the Revolution — Emily was left (as Grace waved goodbye and called out 'Next time') with the lingering feeling that *yes*, they did feel things differently, and that she had, indeed, let a bit of an animal into the house. She dwells on this once again as Gloucester Harbor appears in front of her: a bit of an animal, wise beyond its years.

* * *

It's not the prettiest town on the coast and it never was. It's a working town. A fishing town. Ship building and granite. No, not pretty. A bit scrappy, even, the way working towns are.

It's also a town of stories. Fishing tales, sea tales. All both true and untrue. Fishermen's tales: utterly believable, and fabulous lies. Myths. For it is in working towns like this that mythic memories and tales of the sea are born: memories that survive through successive tellings (each one different from the one before), eventually entering the realm of the mythical and achieving their own truth. The way good tales do. Achieving their own truth to the point that nobody cares any more how they started.

Emily Hale is walking along one of the wharves. It's densely packed with boats and crates and nets drying in the sun; behind her, the lobster and chowder bars the boats supply. On one of his trips back here, after the war, she and Tom walked along the same wharf in sunshine like this. And Tom paused all the way along it, glancing at this boat and that, while taking in the panorama of the whole harbour. And when they reached the end of the wharf he turned round to her, a smile on his face, a light in his eyes, like a man who, after a long journey in foreign lands, was finally home again. Not so much a return of the native, as a rediscovery of home. As if knowing the place for the first time.

A late-morning hush hangs over Gloucester Harbor, broken by occasional talk and shouts. Emily pauses near the end of the wharf. From here she has a good view of the eastern point of the harbour. It's well populated with holiday houses now, but once there was only one house there. Tom's. Or rather, his family's. But she thinks of it as Tom's. She's seen the photographs of the family there (Tom's father lounging on the front veranda), of his brother, sisters and cousins – and Tom, no more than seven or eight years old, playing with a model boat, eyes bright, just like any boy with a new toy. There they lounged, there they sat, there they chatted and laughed or frowned: the family she never had. The photographs a record of summers past. The house would have stood out in those days, before the wood reasserted itself after being cleared and the trees grew back. Up there, amid the boulders and rocks. A lone three-storey residence. Overlooking the harbour, out towards the lighthouse. A clear view of the water, and an easy stroll down to the beach and the jetty where Tom's boat was moored. A catboat. Small, but big enough to take out into the open sea, get into trouble and come back with tales. For as much as he listened to and absorbed the tales of the fishermen, and as much as he thrived on them, he had a tale of his own.

And as she stands there recalling the various tellings, she rubs, even caresses, the satchel strung over her shoulder as if it were a living thing in need of soothing and reassurance. Not long, my dears. Not long. Yes, he had his tale too: a tale told not in the poet's voice or the master's voice or even the Missouri voice (which he always said he lost when he moved east), but told in what she thinks of as Tom's informal, at home voice, rising and falling like the waves as they sat on the boulders, looking out over the harbour ...

One moment he was sailing his boat, summer clouds rolling around in the sky, a distant rumbling every now and then, but no great matter. The air was warm, the boat bobbed up and down on the waves, responding to his touch. Happily. A happy boat on a happy sea. The rocks, the Dry Salvages, were in the distance, teeth bared and clearly visible as he steered his way back towards Gloucester around the headland. A happy boat on a happy sea. Distant rumbling in the summer clouds, but no great matter. All manner of things – boat, birds and man – were well. Warm and pleasant, a day in which to doze. And perhaps he did doze off. Because all was well one minute, and then, it seemed, all was changed.

When the first cold blast hit, the warmth was blown from the air. Still no great matter. Then the second blast of cold air hit, even more suddenly than the first, and not only was the remaining warmth blown away, turning the air winter cold, the light too went from the sky as a giant bank of black cloud rushed in on the wind, blocking out the sun and shutting down the horizon – all as dramatically as a blind being snapped shut. At the same time the catboat's sail blew out and he stood up, trying to rein it in, pulling hard on the ropes, just as the first wave hit with such a massive whack that his knees buckled and he was almost flung overboard. Then the second wave, and the third. The spray, or was it rain, all around. And the boat was propelled forward, no longer bobbing on a happy sea, but blown by an angry one. No longer calm. All changed. And with no warning. A change that no one saw coming. Like those dramatic shifts in temper that turn some people from happy company to spitting vipers in an instant. The same kind of white anger that she knows he is perfectly capable of and which she has witnessed (the white anger that he reserves for her aunt and anybody else guilty of meddling), the same anger that can take the measured and detached, the impersonal Tom Eliot – loftily above the crowd – and fling him into the midst of it, make him just one of the crowd, after all: an incoherent mess of unmastered emotions that blows the Tom Eliot, the T.S. Eliot he presents to the world, into a thousand bits. So too the air and the sea changed. The sail was blown out like a hot air balloon – except he was now drenched and shivering, and the summer flannels he wore so easily just a short time before hung like lead upon him. And the boat, far from bobbing up and down and responding readily to his touch, was being driven through the waves by a maniac wind straight towards the rocks: those granite teeth that were visible one minute, then out of sight – at their most dangerous, lost and submerged under the waves.

And even when he managed to stand on his feet and rein the sail in – a simple task that took all his energy and turned his arms and legs to jelly – the boat was still propelled forward by the wind and the water on an unwavering course that led directly to the rocks, whose gaping teeth – now there, now gone, now there – seemed to be waiting, open-mouthed, for this morsel to arrive. Yet amid it all – the shock of standing in a sea with waves, taller by the minute, hitting the boat one after the other, any one of which could have thrown him into the water – there was still a part of him that was miraculously, or absurdly, detached from it all. Taking notes. A spectator. And while his hands gripped the rudder and he did all he could to steer a safe course, blinded by spray and gulping water, this other, detached part of him, which was observing it all as if not even in the boat but somewhere else, began to look upon the sea as many things. Or did this happen later? Something he added for effect? Probably. All the same, the sea became many things and he had the distinct feeling that he and the boat were being thrown upon the mercy of an angry mob, for suddenly the sea *was* a mob intent on revolution or murder. A mob possessed that saw no distinction between murder and revolution, revolution and murder; driven forward by forces beyond it, which it neither understood nor cared to, towards a blissful violence that it craved and would unleash at the expense of anything that came between that craving and its resolution. The rocks reared up, and the morsel of Tom and his boat was the very sacrifice the god of the rocks required, the mob of the waves intent on delivering him into those waiting jaws.

And as he was registering the mob of the sea, his hands aching on the rudder or frantically trying to work the ropes, the waves rose up with faces, faces from the depths. Waves drawn out in the gusts of wind like a woman's hair, drawn out tight by an invisible hand. And the waves ceased to be an impersonal, nameless and anonymous mob and assumed human faces – all female – drawn up from the depths, all wondrously strange, then strangely recognisable. For these women, it seemed to him at that moment (you must realise, he told her, what moments of such intensity do to the mind), were the faces of the Furies themselves. Furies? Really?

Despite what he said, she wondered then, when he first told her, and she wonders now: don't we make these things up afterwards? And don't we later convince ourselves that this is how it happened? Like those clear memories of events we, in fact, never witnessed? But as much as she wondered about it all then and wonders now, she never said so because he was always so far into the tale by then, his delight in telling it so obvious, and her delight in hearing it such that she didn't care. Let it be, the waves of the sea rose up with women's faces. The Furies. Come for him. And the sea ceased to be indifferent nature – a sheer phenomenon that had fallen on him out of a summer sky – and become something personal. The waves were simply the form the Furies had chosen to take, and this was the destiny they had decided was his. The wind hit him like an assailant; a wave, like a screaming harridan, crashed into the boat, knocking him down – and everything stopped.

Was he really unconscious, had the wind and the wave hit him that hard, or was he spent, exhausted from struggling against a sea bent on his personal destruction? Or did he decide that the forces lined up against him were so overwhelming that struggle was useless, and that all that was left was to lay down his weary frame and pray to a force beyond him, a force commanding enough to overwhelm the sea itself? It was all said to her in the manner of a Kipling tale. Or a sea-going Dickens'. Or both. A performance. For *her*.

And for how long was the world gone? For when he raised his head (was it minutes or seconds?), he had passed the rocks and was being driven into shore, the lighthouse never so welcome, the land never so desired. And when his bobbing cork of a catboat finally rammed into the beach, he lurched into the sand and sank to his knees, whether out of sheer exhaustion or thanks – to that force beyond him to which his weary frame had surrendered, and which had delivered him from the mob and the Furies, and steered him to safety – he didn't know, either then or years later, when he sat on those boulders with Emily, recounting the tale and losing himself in the telling.

And what she saw – and couldn't help but see – was the sheer exhilaration in his eyes as he told it, and which was still there when he finished, on that summer's day not long after the war. But at the same time, she couldn't help but feel that the light in his eyes, the delight, had not so much come from her company as the telling. As though he could have told the same tale to just anybody. Did she know even then that her power was leaving her? That, by then, he'd closed in on himself like a sea creature upon being touched and didn't really want or need anybody any more. Or thought he didn't. And that one day he would utter the fatal words: *too late?*

* * *

Where was she in all of this? Where was Emily? Where was the Miss Hale she eventually became to her 'girls' – for wherever Miss Hale taught, she gathered round her the *crème de la crème* of the senior students, and they became her 'girls'. And she uses that phrase because it is in one of the few contemporary novels she has read – about the prime of a Scottish school teacher, the title of which eludes her, that could so easily have been Emily herself. All through the years of his fame, when she was visiting Tom or he her between the wars, those summers in the same English country town they always went to with her aunt and uncle when Tom was on the run from that fearful woman he married, she either wrote to her girls or shared his letters with them when she returned to America. But only those parts she chose to share, and which she read to them as if they were communications from a distant god, one with whom she just happened to be on first-name terms. It was, she granted, if only to herself, a kind of public confirmation that, as her girls put it, something was 'going on', and *seen* to be going on, between Miss Hale and this distant god, in the same way that the ring that he gave her on one of his visits to the town, and which she no longer wears, was also a confirmation.

But behind the gift of the ring, the letters and the secret references just for her in his poems and essays (transmitted, she always imagined, like coded messages being beamed out from his world to hers), behind all that just what was really going on, or not going on? And how is it that an event that feels as if it is just waiting to happen or already has never does? And where was Emily in all that talk of the storm and the sea and the waves like revolutionary mobs and pursuing Furies, and death and surrender and salvation, and lighthouses never so welcomed, and land never so craved? Who was she? The adventure, or the hearth of the land at the end of the adventure?

She follows the wharf to the end, the eastern point of the harbour stretching out on her left, the house and the boulders upon which they sat concealed by the trees. And as well as having a clear memory of his tale, she also remembers *him* after he told it: quiet, calm, even serene, delighting in the sights and scents of this harbour of his youth; yes, like some modern, everyman Ulysses who had finally come home. For this harbour, the house that overlooks it, the town and the whole coastline, she is sure, was his home. This is where his mythic memories came from, as well as from those childhood years out there in St Louis, before she knew him, where the wide, brown river flowed easily through his dreams and flooded his nightmares: both a kindly god and a terrifying one. Here was his home. And it seemed to her that with every succeeding visit back home he was rediscovering this simple fact. And she could tell him now, as she could have told him then, that wherever you go, Tom, you will always take home with you. It is not just the house and the giant rocks at the front of it that claim you, but the harbour, the pines and this working town that could never be called pretty, but which, all the same, entered your memory and imagination all those years ago, and never let go.

She looks around at the end of the wharf for the right boat, and an old fisherman, one of the locals, emerges from his cabin and waves. The summer sky rumbles. The fisherman, in gumboots and the practical clothes of his trade, shakes her hand and smiles.

'Miss Hale.'

'Henry.'

He drops his hand, she drops hers.

'It's been a while,' he says, noting, she can tell, the changes in her face.

'It has.'

'Have you been well?'

'Well enough.'

'That's all we can ask.'

'Is it?'

There is another pause. The question, bristling with impatience, was directed more at the world than the fisherman, and it goes unanswered.

'Just how long has it been?' Henry frowns.

'It's been years, Henry. Years.'

'Has it now?'

There is another distant rumble and she looks to the sky.

'Will it hold?'

He gives the sky a quick glance. 'Should. It's just a bit of grumbling.'

But it is a judgement offered with a hint of uncertainty, implying that things can change quickly here.

Emily forgets the weather and looks directly at him. 'You heard?'

'Yes.'

He could offer more. She could. But neither of them does. Henry knew Tom all his life. In fact, it was Tom who introduced her to him, almost as if introducing her to a living myth, someone who could just as easily have lived in the distant, early days of the town, and whose stories he had absorbed for years. He was born the same year as Tom, and, she notes, with the faintest trace of amusement, now looks like the Old Man of the Sea himself, but perhaps he is simply one of those, gnarled by constant exposure to the weather, who were always old even when they were young: in the way that Tom, for all his youthful looks, was, in his manner, always an old young man. But as she looks at Henry she decides he has achieved a kind of agelessness, a look that you can't count in years, one that seems to have transcended them.

He met Tom, when they were young, on this wharf. Henry, the fisherman's son; Tom, with a look about him that spoke of money. But all the same, a kid looking for a bit of excitement. Something outside his world. And it was Henry who arranged for Tom to go fishing with them, who introduced Tom to the sea; and Henry who was responsible for Tom's first glimpse of the rocks, coming back in one day from one of those trips that the young Tom never told his parents about. This was a Tom they never knew. And Emily is sure that the Tom Henry knew was another Tom altogether from the one who smoked French cigarettes and read French verse as if, outside of France, he alone understood it. Not her Tom, not his parents' Tom or his brother's or his sisters' Tom – but another one. All housed inside the public Tom. How many Toms were there? How many Emilys?

'Yes, I expected you had.'

Her fingers caress the satchel slung over her shoulder.

'You got my message?'

'I'm here,' he smiles.

'As I am. The two of us.'

And here she lets out a faint sigh and closes her eyes. The slightest betrayal of the emotional forces that have brought her here; the slightest hint that this composed, upright woman in her mid-seventies is not as composed as the world might think, and that she has, indeed, been well enough these last few years – but no more than that.

'Well then,' she says, 'shall we do it? Shall we get the thing done?'

'Yes. No point hanging about. It's the Dry Salvages you want, then?'

'It is.'

'You know we can't go too close?'

'I know.'

'Only fools get too close.'

'Or the foolhardy. Or those who just don't care any more.'

Henry makes no answer, only looks at her with the same uncertainty with which he eyes the sky.

He steps down onto the boat, with its nets and craypots strewn across the deck, for Henry still fishes, still goes out to sea, because – he's said often enough to anyone who'll listen –

what else would he do? And as she points her foot towards the deck he offers to take the satchel from her, but she snatches it back.

'No!'

Her action is swift. Her voice shrill. Why, she seems to be saying, why do you *all* want them?

He is concerned, and wary, taking her hand instead. 'I was just trying to make things easier for you.'

'Oh?' she asks, in a way that suggests there's always something more.

Her mood settles as her feet land on the deck. 'No need, Henry. I can do this.'

She stands there, taking in the residual smells of the morning's catch, of fish and lobster and squid, quietly rebuking herself for the outburst – for just as he heard about the death of Tom on a cold January day earlier in the year, he surely also hears from time to time about Emily: that friends are deserting her, that she took certain things badly and has become what the world calls a 'difficult' woman. Even, depending on whom you talk to, a little bit mad.

Henry loosens the rope securing them to the wharf, and starts the engine. Soon they are moving out, leaving the wharf and the land behind. The wharves and port buildings begin to pass slowly by, the lighthouse awaits. As does the open sea. Out there the Furies ride the surf and the mob of the waves gathers as the sky rumbles.

As they near Eastern Point the lighthouse looms in front of them, white against a swirling, changing sky. The boat, a substantial one built for the open sea, cuts through the swells. Henry, at the wheel, says nothing. Neither does Emily. The silence suits her. Even though she lives only a modest distance away she hasn't seen this coastline for years. Either by accident or on purpose. Or, she ponders, is it accidentally on purpose? It is an annoying phrase to the likes of Emily Hale, and she is annoyed with herself for using it. If only in thought. But, like certain annoying phrases and jingles, it sticks. And she tells herself that whether we like them or not they spring to mind and find speech at the oddest times, and when we do use them, however accidentally, we surrender the moral authority to condemn them. It's like humming one of those songs (pop, they call them) that are everywhere now an hour after you disdained it.

What did her Tom make of this world? This world in which young people seem to be forever running from one place to another. They never seem to walk. That's because they're young, she smiles. And wasn't it always like that? All the same, she can't help but feel that the very fact that *everything* is young now — on the television and at the cinema and on the covers of tacky, coloured magazines that bulge from newsstands like bunches of plastic flowers — is odd. Even suspicious. As though somebody has only just discovered that youth has money and will pay to see itself up there on television screens and on magazine covers. And so youth itself, she imagines, becomes not only the subject of television programs and magazine articles, but the product as well. Is *that* what's different, or was it always like that? She doubts it. This is a different kind of youth.

What did he make of this world? She'll never know because she never had the chance to ask him. They'd stopped seeing each other, talking to each other and writing to each other by then – when the world, abruptly, turned young and she felt not only deserted and alone, but quite old. As though all the expectation and the waiting for Tom had somehow kept her young. But once there was nothing left to wait for, once she'd lost him for the second time, once he was irrevocably gone from her life and all the waiting had come to nothing, that which had sustained her left her. And it was during this time that she first felt herself to be, and pronounced herself, a spinster. A hateful word that conjured up images of ugly women in fairy tales. And as much as she told herself not to use it, she did. It was, she concluded, due to a sort of self-contempt, as though she had failed in some way, and the whole long wait for nothing in the end was her fault. And the more she told herself it wasn't, the more she denied the charge of spinsterhood (as though delivered by a ghostly chorus of long-dead aunts), the more it fell upon her, as though it was her destiny, all she deserved. She had waited, in parlour and garden, all her life. And in the end, all her waiting had come to nothing.

She looks round at the shoreline and watches as the lighthouse slowly recedes. The previous year, in late summer or the fall, she'd watched on television the arrival in New

York of a group of young musicians who looked vaguely like French intellectuals, but who spoke in interviews with a strong northern English accent that she knew well from her travels. Not from the village in which she nearly always met Tom, but from trips further north. Taken to fill in time while Tom wasn't around or to be near Tom while he gave a lecture or a reading. And always, more or less, his secret – the secret Miss Hale who wasn't there, who was only spoken of in trusted circles. But when he wasn't in the village or back in London, she explored the rest of the country. Often the north. And so she felt a certain connection with these young musicians, as though she and they had something in common. Felt a surprising affection, even. For they brought with them – in their very voices – echoes and hints of a place and time when the waiting was as real as the possibility of the dreams of dreaming waves coming true.

It was the only time she's ever felt any genuine connection with this new world, for their voices conjured up her past. And it's not as though she finds this new world confusing or baffling. It's just not hers any more. And for the first time in her life she's beginning to think that you can live too long.

From time to time Henry looks round for her, almost as though he's checking she's still there. As though he's read her thoughts. And there she is, clutching that damn satchel and whatever is in it, riding the jolts of the waves and looking out to sea like some sailor's widow, even though there's nothing left to wait for.

Is that what he sees? Why not? It's what she herself sees at this moment. And the thought that you can live too long returns. But it's not frightening. No. There's something comfortably logical, even symmetrical, she imagines, about beginnings, middles and, yes, endings, that makes death ... *do-able.*

4.

There's really only one main street in the town, and not much to look at there anyway. Not for the likes of Grace and Ted. But there is a music shop. There are music shops everywhere now, because music is everywhere. They are standing at the front window of the shop, gazing at an electric guitar. They have been for a while. Ted is dreaming out loud, telling her just what he could do with a guitar like that if he only had the money to buy it, and Grace is nodding, but only half listening.

It's morning, bright and sunny, and a short time ago Grace watched Miss Hale drive along the main street and out of town. She knew it was Miss Hale at a glance. That car. You couldn't mistake it. And as Ted is talking, she rubs the love bite on her neck, Miss Hale's small lounge room appearing before her as she does: the old furniture, the paintings and framed qualifications on the walls, and the sideboard built from the kind of dark red wood that tells you it's expensive. And on top of the sideboard, framed snaps of people and faces, young then but old now, like the furniture. Or dead. And one of the snaps she knows is important. She knows this one, above all the others, is important, because she caught Miss Hale looking at it one day during her lesson. And not just casually, but puzzled and lost in it. To the point that when she looked up and saw Grace she was momentarily surprised by her presence, then regained herself.

And Grace is thinking of the man in that photograph now as Ted goes on and on about the guitar. He's somebody famous, very famous, she knows that. Miss Hale is one of those women that a town like this talks about. And it's well known that she and somebody famous had a thing. Or almost had a thing. And Grace, with the unerring accuracy of the young (who don't appear to be noticing anything around them, but who are taking in everything), has long concluded that this oldish-looking man with a part down the middle of his hair, and who looks so English, is that someone famous. But she's never got around to asking just who he is, for a number of reasons. Mostly because it's Miss Hale's business. Had she ever asked and had Miss Hale ever replied 'That's Tom. Tom Eliot', it still wouldn't have meant anything. It's not 'Tom' that makes the name Eliot distinctive, it's the 'T.S.'. She's heard of T.S. Eliot, a sort of Shakespeare. He's on her 'should read' list. One day. A kind of duty, like Shakespeare. But she hasn't read him and has never seen a photograph of him. Or if she has, she wouldn't have known who it was. No, all she hears about is this 'special friend', this 'companion', and while she knows it's code for someone famous, she's never known who. But she's also never asked about the photograph because, in his tweed suit, tweed cap, short pants and long socks (leaning against what is unmistakeably Miss Hale's car), he looks like a golfer. And whenever she looks at the photograph or occasionally, for no particular reason, thinks of that room, she sees this golfer. And who asks about golfers? Only her father. And so, over the months that she's been going to Miss Hale, she's come to think of him as this golfer: this famous golfer that Miss Hale once had a thing with.

There are times when she doesn't mind being in that room: the lessons pass the time and she does get something from them. And there are other times when she just can't wait to get out, as if she were suffocating. Just as there are times when she likes Miss Hale, quite likes her – and other times when she wants to shake her and shake her until something like the real Miss Hale finally pipes up and she drops the whole nineteenth-century Henry James thing altogether. And although she has never read T.S. Eliot, Grace has read Henry James. Even likes him. Sort of fell into him one classically rainy afternoon. *Washington Square.* She lives just off Washington Square, was automatically drawn to the book because of the title, and after reading it was haunted by the characters and that whole world of Henry James for weeks. It's one of the things that she and Miss Hale have in common, one of those things that spans the ages between them and gives Grace a way of picturing Miss Hale in her time and place – something that makes her understandable. Turns Miss Hale into a kind of Catherine, forever waiting. Not that she's ever mentioned this to her. No, she might like James, but she has no desire to live her life as if having been written by him.

But Miss Hale — and the name says it all — seems to. Whether she knows it or not. And rather than have a discussion with Miss Hale about James, she'd like to shake Henry James right out of her and see what's left. If anything.

Then Ted asks her something and she's wrenched from Miss Hale's lounge room and is back on the street.

'It's a beauty. What do you think?'

She shrugs, he turns back to the window. Ted's not his real name. It's actually Waldo, or Humphrey, or something that belongs in a circus. And he wasn't having that, so he called himself Eddie. After one of those Eddies from the fifties. And soon everybody shortened it to Ted. And that was that. She's eighteen, he's twenty-two. Only four years difference, but there are times when his fifties feel as distant to her as Miss Hale's Boston tales, in those glimpses she gives of her youth, where the real Miss Hale, no doubt, was left behind.

Grace is from New York. Her father is a lecturer. Sociology. Weber, except you say *V*aber. He's here in New England for six months, five of which are up, before they go back to New York. Her mother disappeared with another academic years before. Philosophy. Kant. Except you say … Well, the joke (according to her father) was that he *couldn't* bring himself to say it. She grins. He would say that. Her mother and her philosopher disappeared somewhere into New Zealand. Have been there for years, and she rarely hears from her, let alone sees her. She tells herself that she never really knew her (she was two years old when she left) and you can't miss what you've never had. But all her friends tell Grace that as soon as she turns thirty – on the stroke of midnight – she's going to crumble into a screaming heap and call for her mama.

She's finished high school and come September she'll go to university. Which one they're not sure, because she only just scraped through high school. All the same, she told Miss Hale one day that she was going to Harvard in the fall, and a look of envy and longing came instantly into Miss Hale's eyes. And the meaning of the look was clear: that was never possible in my time. You young people, with your freedoms and your love bites. She never said this, of course. But she didn't have to. And Grace added that she didn't want to go to Harvard or Princeton or Yale or Rutgers – and she pronounced them all with a sort of jaunty, bouncing rhythm – all she wanted to do was sing in a band. And she knows she can sing, really sing (it's been confirmed by Miss Hale), better than most of the singers in the bands she hears on records. But her father insists she find a university, get a degree and *then* she can sing her heart out. And when she said this, Miss Hale took on a sympathetic look that said, you and I ... we might not be so different, after all. At least, it looked like that.

So this is all a kind of in-between time for Grace. And when they first came to the town she couldn't believe she'd last a week, let alone six months. There was nothing, nothing to do. Then she met Ted. Well, she had to eventually. Small town. Big history, but small town. And she knew straight away that he was one of those who are always two steps behind the times.

But he had a touch of excitement about him. Danger, even. A bit of an animal. Been in trouble with the police. Did a job once. Nothing much. Break-in, a few dollars. He shrugged it off when he told her as though everyone did it. But apart from this, one of the things that Ted had going for him was that he had a car (he does deliveries). That and his looks. Dark eyes. The brooding eyes of a poet, except he's not a poet's bootlace. But he's got the looks. The right looks at the right time. And this, she knows already, is one of those times in her life she will occasionally look back on and pause for a while, when she's old enough to start looking back. And although Grace was sort of imprisoned in a small town, with her father at work all day, she also had more freedom or, rather, the chance for more freedom than she'd known before. And a car was freedom. And Ted, she could tell, would be fun enough. A phase, she smiles to herself as she points to something on the guitar and asks what it is. Her Ted phase.

'It's the tremolo arm,' he says.

She's heard of tremolo arms, pretty much in the same way as she's heard of Frank Sinatra. And as she looks at the guitar, Ted all excited and jumpy like a fifteen-year-old, she can see straight away that it's yesterday's guitar. The kind of guitar that was always strung around the necks of yesterday's singers. The old singers, all those forgotten Eddies, played guitars like this. No one plays them any more, not on television. That's why it's going cheap. And with that thought, she is also aware once again of the gap between them. Not just in years, but everything else. Sometimes the difference between one decade and the one that follows can be as dramatic as a shift in generations. And to Grace, the difference between the fifties and the sixties is one of those shifts. Suddenly, Elvis was an old fart. And overnight. How often does that happen? And as Ted stands in front of yesterday's guitar, all jumpy and excited, it's the eighteen-year-old Grace who feels the older of the two. And there's sadness in his excitement, for she knows that this is Ted's lot, Ted's life: two steps behind the times, and getting excited over yesterday's guitar.

'If I had the money I'd buy it now. Just walk right in and walk right out strumming it. Would you like that?'

'I would,' she laughs. That's the other thing about Ted, he makes you laugh. Yes, she would like to see it. And she means it. It's impossible not to get caught up in his enthusiasm. For it's got a kind of innocence to it that'll never go. He'll be fifty, she thinks with amusement, and still be saying things like that. And with that thought comes a wave of affection for Ted, or for herself and all her friends who will wake one day and be fifty. She'll just have to imagine Ted at fifty, because she won't be there. And as much as it's yesterday's guitar and yesterday's dream, she wants him to have it because, heaven knows, for all the life and fun that Ted's got in him, life isn't going to give him much fun in return. Especially when that brushed-back hair thins, for Ted was born to go bald.

'Money.' He stands there shaking his head. 'It's always getting in the way.'

'The money'll come along.'

'How?'

'It always does,' she shrugs.

He laughs at this, more of a snort really: it always does for *you*, he might have said, and she is waiting for him to say it, but he doesn't. They leave the music shop and walk along the street to the only diner in the town. At least, the only diner worth bothering with. She looks at him, lost in thought. Yes, she reminds herself, dark eyes. Good arms too. All those deliveries. And she rubs her neck where the love bite is. Bit of an animal. Her Ted phase.

And today there's more to Ted than his looks and his bounce and his car. Today, and he doesn't say how, he's got his hands on some dope. Grass. Not much, but enough for the both of them to find out what the fuss is all about.

They step into the diner. Breakfast is finishing, a waitress is collecting the plates. There is a song on the jukebox, one she has heard all through the summer, for it is clearly somebody's favourite. And although there is a jangling guitar all through it that marks it out as a song of its times, there is also something about this song, in which the singer is telling somebody to lay down their weary tune in much the same way that you might tell a soldier to lay down his gun or a warrior his sword, there is something about this song that belongs to no particular time at all. As if it's written by nobody in particular. Blown in on the wind. It fades, it finishes. They sit and drink their coffee. They talk of the guitar, money, and if it's going to come along as it always does, where from? And all the time they are talking, young people she has vaguely got to know, mostly students like her on holiday, are feeding the jukebox in the corner, sustaining one of the few things in town worth their coins.

5.

Emily Hale is not a woman given to impulsive daring – or surrendering to its wondrous or awful consequences. But one day in the spring of 1927, by then teaching in Wisconsin, she sat down to write a letter. And just as a night of amateur theatre had changed her life fourteen years before, so too did this letter.

Tom Eliot, *her* Tom (always remembered with the same face he had when he left), had become, in the intervening years, T.S. Eliot. He had entered the years of fame. Studio photographs in bookshops now displayed this other Tom, this T.S. Eliot who stared back at you with a look that was somewhere between a university don's (which he almost became) and a bank manager's. Yes, he had entered the years of fame, had written the poem that had become the anthem of a generation, had acquired a public face and – she read from time to time in journals and newspapers, or simply heard from mutual acquaintances who'd visited him – a precise, clipped voice and a distant manner that said you may come so far only, but no closer. In short, he was on the way to becoming a great man of letters, on the way to becoming that public figure who would, in time, learn to hide himself in plain view. Which made picking up the pen to write to him that day all the more daunting.

But as much as he had become known and found a kind of fame, he had, it seemed, also found deep unhappiness. Or was it that unhappiness was the price of fame and had found him? For those mutual acquaintances who had visited him (old college friends Emily had met from time to time) also came back speaking of this unhappiness and his marriage to a woman who had the reputation of being fearsome and demanding. At least, these were the reports she chose to believe and draw strength from.

Had the marriage been happy, would she have lifted the pen to write that letter? Probably not. And the marriage itself, she'd heard, so sudden. Almost furtive. One week, it seemed, he was sending Emily yellow roses, delivered by a mutual Boston friend; the next he was married.

Over a year after Tom had left for Oxford, she was sitting in Boston Common one morning, the warm June weather having drawn her outdoors. She was contemplating the luminosity of the leaves and the lawns, and the various coffee, doughnut and hotdog stands around her. Even contemplating buying a hotdog smothered in mustard, for she had never had one. That too was beneath her. And while she was contemplating this, as if the hotdog were some exotic tropical fruit, deciding that she would, she *must* taste it (and let Tom know by letter her reaction, for it was the sort of thing he loved to hear about), a figure loomed in front of her, momentarily blocking the sun.

'Emily,' a young woman was saying, a school friend she had kept in contact with and saw from time to time. 'Emily Hale. What are you doing, hanging round a public park all alone?'

'Contemplating a hotdog.'

Laughter was in the air. The young woman plopped onto the park bench beside Emily, and they fell into talk of this teacher and that old school friend and what had become of them all since they went their different ways. And at some point the young woman turned to her, rested her hand on Emily's arm and said, 'Oh, and your friend! What a shock.'

Emily was still smiling. 'Which friend? What shock?'

The young woman's face darkened. '*Your* friend.'

'Who?'

'Tom. Tom Eliot. Don't you know?'

'Clearly not.' Emily was still unconcerned, her eyes still bright. But the frown on her old school friend's face changed that.

'You really don't?'

The lightness left her and her mind was racing. Had there been an accident? Was he ill? Good heavens, had he died and no one told her?

'What are you saying?'

The young woman looked out over the common and raised her eyebrows, clearly wishing she'd never mentioned the matter, then looked directly at Emily. 'He's married.'

She caught only the odd phrase here and there over the next few minutes before the young woman rose and left her; strolling away over a carpet of green and under a canopy of luminous branches. Married? And married to someone nobody had ever heard of, an English woman. All very sudden, her friend had said, an observation delivered with the hint of a suggestion. In a registry office at some ungodly hour of the morning. Didn't even tell his parents. Thought, the woman added before leaving, he would have told you.

Emily was looking at the receding figure of her old school friend but, in fact, had barely noted her departure. She was gazing blankly out over the common: the colour, the sounds, the comings and goings of the scene – no concern to her now – hardly registering. *Married?* How *can* that be? Surely, there was a mistake. But of course, there wasn't. How had this happened? She here; Tom there. Somebody had come along, after all. It had to happen. Of course. Evil Europe. Everything is different here, he might have written. But he gave no hint. And how plain, how ordinary, how *un*-destined Emily must have looked from over there. And Boston, Cambridge and parlour stunt shows now part of a world made small by distance. Along with Emily herself. Small-town Emily, whom he was always going to leave when the right somebody came along. And that somebody had.

She's not sure how long she sat looking, blank-eyed, over the common. At some point she became aware of the hotdog stand again, its irrelevant smell carrying to her on a gentle breeze. But she'd lost the taste for exotic fruit. And the letter to Tom that she'd fancifully planned – outlining her responses to the taste of mustard and hotdog, as well as all the funny little ways of the hotdog vendor, which she felt sure would have amused him – would never be written now.

At some point she rose and drifted away over the common, a different Emily from the one who had entered it not so long ago, but long enough to mark the difference between one life and another.

The roses stopped coming, communication ceased. All smiles stopped together. Sending her roses one week – and slipped from her life the next. All of which, over the following weeks, brought back that early impression she had of him: that there just might be something ungrounded in Tom Eliot, a flaw in the crystal, a crack in the otherwise perfect social construction that only became evident at certain times, such as surrendering to the awful, the impulsive daring of a hasty marriage. Sneaking off at six in the morning to a registry office and telling virtually no one.

But when she picked up the pen to write her letter that day in faraway Wisconsin, she was also asking herself if she was any different. If anybody is. We all, she told herself, we all have those cracks in our nature and we have no right to expect otherwise of someone else. Even if in their dress, manner and speech, they invite such expectation. And as much as she felt he had let himself down, let *her* down, she also concluded that everybody was allowed one reckless mistake. And it was this crack, along with his deep unhappiness (confirmed by report after report of returning friends and acquaintances), that made him more approachable that day. So she wrote: a silly excuse of a letter that was vaguely embarrassing at the time but which she rationalised was plausible enough all the same. She was teaching at a girls school, teaching drama; could he recommend some reading? A little embarrassing, but she posted it anyway, expecting only a formal reply, if, indeed, there were one at all.

But the reply was fast. Leaping with delight. A springtime letter from a friend who would, in a short space of time, once more become her 'special friend'. Her 'companion'. And when reading excerpts from his letters over the succeeding years to her girls at various schools, she would always refer to him as her 'special friend' in a way that implied that, indeed, something was going on between Miss Hale and the great man. And so her daring was rewarded, and she gradually entered the life of her Tom once again: entered the years of his fame, but silently and invisibly so. Known only to a small circle of friends. By his side, but for all the world not there at all. She couldn't be. He was married, and she *was* Miss Hale.

They have left the lighthouse and Eastern Point behind them now and are facing the open sea. The waves are choppy, the sharp tang of the sea and the cry of gulls are all around her and the idea of the 'open' sea, of sailing out into a world without boundaries, makes sense in this small fishing boat far more than it ever did on any of the ocean liners that took her from Boston to Tom and back again over the years. Above her the clouds are gathering, the rumbling continues. And as she looks around, Henry calls out, asking if she's game. Should they continue or come back another day? She shakes her head firmly, indicating her desire to press on, as a wave smacks against the side of the boat and she grabs the railing. Henry raises his eyebrows and turns back to the wheel, disappointed, she can't help but feel. Not because he's wary of the weather, but wary of her.

And so she entered the years of his fame. Letters became visits, Atlantic crossings, she to him and he to her. Letters became visits, and visits eventually became the ring that he gave her, which she no longer wears. But she was kept a secret. There, but not there. Known only to a few of Tom's friends. The inner circle. For he was not only a public poet by then, but a married one. Separated, on the run. But married, all the same.

And she knew what they thought of her, that inner circle (or most of them), right from the start. Nice, they thought. Warm, the way old flames are warm. Matronly. Just what Tom needed. But no match for him the way that fearsome wife of his was. No match for their Tom. For he had become theirs by then – English passport, English church and just a bit too solemn – and she was found wanting. Straight away. The tall, thin figure of Mrs Woolf seems to loom in front of her, standing opposite Emily in the boat, curling a comb of honey, passing her a tea-cup; Tom beside her; Mr Woolf (a marmoset on his shoulder); and that boyish young poet who said profound things – all gathering around her now as they did when she and Tom visited them. A strained hour or two. And all the time Mrs Woolf staring into her from the mask of her face, smoking with practised languidness, annoying her the way Tom's French cigarettes always annoyed her, and Emily having to keep up this constant, measured conversation about things that seemed to matter awfully to them (from questions about whether American Indians mingled with society to earnest inquiries about the Santa Fe trail, as if they intended to go there, which they clearly didn't). And because she couldn't let Tom down, she had to pretend it all mattered to her. But once outside their house, she could drop the pretence of caring about matters of absolutely no consequence to her or, she strongly suspected, to anybody else in the room that afternoon. It was talk, talk, talk. And all the time their eyes boring deep into her from the masks of their faces. And at one point, a strong urge to wipe the posed complacency off their faces – Mrs Woolf's, Mr Woolf's and that boyish poet's – rose up in her. For she knew exactly what they thought. At least Tom's wife, they would have thought but never said, fearsome and exhausting as she is, is interesting, but not so Tom's Boston bore, refined beyond enduring, who would, no doubt, quickly become in all their minds that 'awful American woman', or something like it. The masks of their faces said nothing, but their eyes said it all.

And did Tom notice any of this? He didn't seem to, but he must have. No, they never said as much, but they didn't have to. Not that it mattered. Not really. She had her Tom back, or what was left of him; that was all that mattered. Mrs Woolf fades from view with a regal wave of the hand, as if releasing her. The company that day – Mr Woolf, the marmoset and the profound poet – also fade from the scene, leaving her standing on the deck of the boat with that distinct sensation of having been found wanting all over again. A wave smacks the side of the boat; a large white bird, too big to be a gull, swoops, plunges beneath the water and emerges with its wriggling prey in its beak. She was back in Tom's world, and he was in hers, and most summers from then on they passed together under the same sky, be it England's or New England's – that was all that mattered and all she cared about.

He had once offered himself to her, not in so many words, but she knew he had and she knew she *had* him, on a string even, but because she was annoyed with the world that day she never gave him the confirmation he came for, and which showed him that his affections were returned. Then he left and the string snapped. But, surely, life had given them a second chance, and she could return those affections after all, after all that had happened, and they could begin again.

She frowns and shifts her gaze to the sky. What fools we are. The sky rumbles in the distance, and she walks about the deck unsteadily, clutching the satchel. What fools we are. Emily, Emily, why couldn't you see it coming? Or could you, but didn't want to? Or even care to? Emily, Emily … Another wave slaps the boat and she stumbles, almost dropping the satchel.

'Are you sure about this?' Henry calls.

'Yes! Will you stop asking?'

Her voice has the same edge as when she stepped onto the boat. Shrill, she notes, the voice of a 'difficult' woman. Henry shakes his head, the same puzzled wariness in his eyes and a look that suggests: I do this for old times. Her gaze shifts to the sea and the circling gulls. Emily, Emily, that's what you get for being a little fool. You handed over your *life*, you little fool. Was that how it happened? See only what you want. Is that how these things unfold? You reach a point, without realising it, when going back and going forward are the same; when you no longer control events, events control you. That's what hope does. Feeds you the story you want to believe. Except it's not a story, it's your life. You should have seen it in those first visits: the picture postcard town, not quite real; Tom, not quite real; and you, Emily, the secret he rushed to meet.

There they were; there they are. Emily wearing the summer dress she'd worn only a short while ago in the bright golden sunshine of California where, by then, she taught, and Tom in those tweedy English things that he wore in that postcard town, the type of clothes that people relaxed in when they got away from things. But Tom was like an old spring that disintegrates upon being touched. There they were; and are. California sun one day, Midlands the next. Same clothes. Not quite real. Nothing quite real. And Tom, ready to snap.

* * *

'Tom, you remember we agreed to watch together for that great event you were so fearful of missing?'

'Yes,' he says wearily, nodding slowly and looking down, with a lean, it seems, like the tower of Pisa: once tall and proud, now barely able to support his frame. She shakes her head slowly, gazing at him: what have they done to you?

They are walking down the main street of the Cotswold town to which she has come for the first time for the summer: the town he has come up to from London to meet her. A pretty town. The kind of town they put in tourist brochures and Baedekers and on posters. Her aunt and uncle have one cottage. She has the smaller, adjacent one. And when Tom comes up he stays next door with her aunt and uncle. That way nobody is compromised. All very proper. All the way it should be. Will she ever be allowed to forget he is a married man? At least, walking the streets or through the surrounding fields, they are left to themselves.

'Has it finally announced itself, this great event?'

And even as she asks the question, with more urgency and impatience than she intended, she is also silently addressing him: why, why can't you just say it, Tom? After all this time. Just *say* it, say that love, love is the great event.

'Yes and no.'

A van rumbles up the high street in the late-afternoon sun. Rooftops and stone archways begin to glow. A flock of birds rises musically into the air and settles again. It is the very best time to be out. Now and in the mornings, watching the town come to postcard life.

'Has it happened? Do you feel it has?'

He is distracted, not quite there: an intricate mechanism about to explode or shut down. Or simply fall down, a tower that leans once too often. Speech is an effort. Words wobble from his lips. 'Yes, it has happened. And is happening again, only differently. Not the way one imagined it.'

They pause at a market stall, closing for the day. *One?* Who is this *one?* And who does he think he's talking to? An audience? She wants to shake him and say, Tom, it's me, *me* you are talking to. Poultry, local fish, vegetables and fruit are arranged on a table like a still life. Not quite real. And she wouldn't be surprised if they weren't. A few stalls away, the young woman, Catherine, who cleans the cottages, is kissing her young man. A market-stall kiss, oblivious of everyone. No sense of being watched, no parlour-room manners, just this way of *living*, this ease with themselves and the world that Emily has never known. That Tom's never had. And wouldn't everything have been better right from the start if they'd had that ease, that way of living that stops at market stalls and kisses, oblivious of the watching world. She turns slowly to him as the two young people move on.

'And was it love? Was it love all along?'

He frowns, concentrating, then slowly shakes his head as if the whole matter were beyond him. 'Yes and no. No, and yes. I barely know what I mean or what I want any more, if I want anything.'

She pauses, summoning the right tone and rolling the whole of her life into her question. 'Is it still there, or have we missed it?'

He doesn't answer, only looks at her as if to ask where they should walk to from here. To amble through the streets of the town or take their usual path, down to the stream and on to the pathway through the wheat fields that will be golden in the afternoon sun. And she returns the look, as if asking the same question but with a different meaning: indeed, Tom, where to from here?

'It was, at least, what I then thought of as love. What I took to be love.'

'And which you now don't?'

He squints into the distance, fragile, drained of life, and it's not hard to imagine him old. In fact, he's already looking it. For he is one of those who even as a young man had an older way. Both a young old man and an old young man. But the Tom beside her is something else: just plain haggard, sagging eyes, pale drawn face, someone to whom the world has become frightening. And if she did not have the picture-perfect memory of Tom as he was before he ever left, she would never have been able to see the young Tom inside the old. If he'd passed her in the street, would she have known him? For a moment, the pain that comes with this question makes her look quickly away, hovering on the brink of tears. What have they done to you, what have they *done*?

'I am, quite simply, not the me I was then. And what I felt as love then, I can't now.' His voice is almost gravelly, the words dragged from him. 'So much has happened.'

And as he stares at her, the darkest eyes she's ever looked into, his face, his expression, his very demeanour have the look of someone to whom, indeed, much has happened. And she knows, as does he, exactly what he means – just what this something that has happened is. And although she has never before broached the business of his marriage, for fear of meddling or intruding on territory that is not hers to intrude upon, she now does.

'Your marriage? You mean your marriage?'

He is so thin, leaning towards her, almost collapsible. 'Yes,' he sighs, 'and what I once felt as love, I can't any more.' He pauses, then adds, 'When I received your letter – and it was a beautiful spring morning, the kind of morning on which one could imagine falling in love – it made me feel the way I felt as a young man. Almost. And I went through the day believing I was a young man again. And that falling in love as the young do was once more a possibility. But it wasn't. I am not that young man. Nor will ever be again. And what I once felt as love I knew I couldn't feel any more. Too much had happened.'

And he stands before her with an expression that says, what have we done? What have *I* done? I'm not what I was and never will be again. And he looks down at his frame, his arms and legs and feet, as if disgusted. As if some contamination has entered his organs and veins and needs to be expelled –

expelled and expunged before he can move on. And as pleadingly haunted as his expression is, it is one that also asks, who can help me? Can *nobody*?

And it is at this moment, standing on the edge of the town square in the fading light, staring into those helpless and *un-helpable* eyes, that she registers, more dramatically than she has ever done before, the damage that has, indeed, been done. For here is no great man, peering down at you, imperious and all-knowing, from the insides of books or from bookshop walls, but a deeply damaged one. No mind of Europe to be seen there, just a haunted look. Can *nobody* help me? And not so much a refined sensitivity that caught the disillusion of an entire generation and their times, and which made him both famous and miserable, as a raw one. Exposed. Painful to touch. A man without skin, or illusions. And who doesn't seem to know where to turn. And she knows, with equal certainty, that whatever fanciful thoughts she may have entertained of perhaps this ... and one day, perhaps that ... they are a fairy tale that will never be lived. That her Tom is gone, and whatever it is that they can now share will be utterly different from anything she, or they, ever imagined.

'When I talk of love,' he says, unaware of any break in the conversation, 'I don't mean love the way most people think of it.'

He is frowning. His face is troubled. Almost contorted. This is difficult. No, what do the English say at such moments? Awkward! If she had a smile in her right now she would smile. But he's not English, as much as he tries to be. And for a moment it seems this is all he is going to say. For how many times has he done this to her? Said just so much, and then left the matter hanging? No, her look says, you owe me more than that, Tom. Not again. Say it! The thing that has to be said. I deserve this much. Say it!

Glancing at her, reading, she knows, her thoughts (and it can't be difficult, for she is sure she makes herself understood with remarkable, even bold, clarity), he continues, gazing out across the market square, the stalls now being dismantled.

'You have to understand,' and again he is halted by this anguished awkwardness, 'how it was.'

He falls silent. She lets him be. There is almost a smile on his face when he resumes. 'Like being in a Dostoyevsky novel, written by your uncle John.'

Her face falls. Oh, dear. Is that all? Is that it? And I thought it was *my* Tom speaking. Or what is left of him. Tom speaking to Emily. But it's only T.S. Eliot. With a cheap line that he thinks is a good one. When this is no time for lines at all. Cheap or otherwise. But perhaps, she's now thinking, that although she knows the Tom of their youth, underneath there's always been this utterly driven Tom that she's never known. A Tom that, quite possibly, no one has ever known. And again, her look signals the sheer inadequacy of what he has just said.

It is a conversation, she thinks, of truths and half-truths, of honesty and cheapness, speech and silence. But when he resumes, almost apologetically making amends for cheap lines, it is her Tom speaking again.

'I feel drained. Emptied.' And again he looks down at the frame, the arms, legs and feet that so disgust him. 'Nothing left. As if I've had the life sucked out of me. Not by Vivienne ...'

The mention of her name coincides with the clapper-board snap of a dismantled stall hitting the ground. But it is not just the coincidence that makes the moment clap like thunder. It is, remarkably, the first time he has ever spoken her name. And he utters it as though he can barely bring himself to say it. As though speaking her name confirms the reality of the nightmare. And that they are, however much they may be physically separated, still joined. Coupled. An acknowledgement that she will always claim him, that they will always be bound, and that the past will never be vanquished. That the past will always be present, now and in the future.

'No ... not just Vivienne.'

She notes there is care in the way he says her name this time, and it is also at this moment that Emily realises, with painful certainty, that he once loved her. Must have. For there is a tenderness in the way he says her name that speaks of love; that speaks of times in which they shared things, moments that were theirs and theirs only, which she cannot and will never know. And as much as she might imagine him as *her* Tom, he became, all those years before when she wasn't there and while she wasn't watching, somebody else's Tom. And would now always be somebody else's Tom, as much as hers. There was somebody else Tom once loved, in that moment of reckless surrender; loved enough to rush off to a registry office with in the early hours of a weekday morning to seal their unhappy fate.

'Not by Vivienne.' And here he speaks her name not only with gentle care, but as if speaking of some fantastic, highly gifted child, who tried so very hard to grow up and grow into the world in such a way that she wasn't a bother to everyone, but who, in the end, couldn't find a way. And this surge of tenderness, this repetition of her name, reverberates in Emily's ears, leaving her momentarily wavering on her feet. 'No, not by Vivienne ... but by the thing itself. What we did to each other,' he proclaims, his voice rising with every word that follows. 'What *I* did! And as much as I might tell myself that it was a nightmare we both created and that nobody was to blame, I don't believe it. Not where it matters.'

Again he stares back at her, helpless and un-helpable. His words seemingly echoing around the square. It is a look that asks, where to from here? Forward, yes. But which way is that?

'So,' he continues, his voice soft again, 'when I speak of love now it is not in the same way most people do. And I wish it weren't true. I wish, for all the world, that I could just be that young man falling in love as everybody else does on a spring morning made for love. But he's gone. The life drained out of him. Do you know what it is like to lose the desire for all the things you once *so* desired?'

'No,' she says, 'I've never lost it.'

'No.' And he gazes out over the square slowly emptying itself of produce, trade and commerce. 'I'd like to be able to say that too. I would like to be able to say that very much. But I can't. And so when I speak of love, I mean another kind. Quite possibly my only salvation. But one you may find, I have no doubt, very difficult. Difficult and demanding. I'm not even sure I can be salvaged,' he says, his voice rising again. 'Sometimes, I feel it's something between God and me.'

Emily is a religious woman, but, there is something in the way he mentions God – in the same way that he speaks of Coleridge and me, of Wordsworth and me – that's just a bit too solemn and self-appointed and leaves her uneasy. Even annoyed. And as if picking up on this, his tone becomes brisk. 'Go. Go, Emily! Get out of here! Get out of this whole situation as fast as you can. I'm a wreckage. A walking mess. I'm no good to anybody. Go. Go, Emily!'

He seems to be hovering on the brink of tears or collapse or both. And it is like watching that perfectly composed figure that smiles all-knowingly and benevolently down upon you in the bookstores break down. Fragment. And crumple. The pose, the public face behind which he hides in clear sight, shattered. The all-knowing eyes knowing nothing. And he either steps forward or simply falls against her, but all at once she is feeling the full weight of him. A fallen tower. He says nothing, nor does she. She is simply registering the blissful burden that has fallen on her. Her Tom, back again. Or what is left of him. For he is reaching out – to her. To Emily. Can *nobody* help me? And with the collision of his speaking her name, the sight of those helpless and un-helpable eyes and the jolt of taking the full weight of him, she knows that she will, that she must, receive that wreckage. That mess. It is decided in an instant, as if having already happened. And will again.

'Do you understand what I am asking?' he says, when he has finally composed himself and stands upright on his own feet again.

'Yes.'

And she does. Oh, yes she does. Not a love that pauses brazenly by a market stall and kisses, oblivious of the watching world, not a coupling like beasts in the field, but the love of two people who will be *there* for each other. Held together by the memory of what they were, the great strength of untouchable, old love that ennobles the human beast. And was it in this moment that the 'Lady of silences' was born: the Lady who watches, who forgives and who saves, but who cannot be touched. They are on a knife-edge. The world has become a frightening place to Tom. He is a man to whom the Furies are real.

'Go. Go, Emily. It is unfair. I have no right to ask. To involve you. Nobody does.'

And for a moment she is, indeed, asking herself just what she is getting involved in. But she will, and she must. For she was always involved. And it was always going to happen like this. The matter was decided long ago. 'It's not a question of being fair or right.'

'What I ask, it's not ... not normal. Not what the world understands as love.'

'No, it's not.'

She says this without censure. No, Tom. It's not. What you're asking is what the world might call abnormal. But we're not the world, are we? We're not the world, we're us. And an exquisite thrill runs through her, for however less than satisfactory this 'us' may be, it is, all the same, 'us'. And perhaps, for the time being, they can discover together this other kind of love. And perhaps this will sustain them until her Tom is salvaged from the wreckage he has become, and what remains of the bruised body and the bruised soul is finally returned to him and to her. And through that, in time, they may find that ordinary, everyday love that just anybody can know. Perhaps. 'No, it's not. And I'm not even sure we can do this thing. But …'

He winces, almost as though he wishes he'd never spoken and never asked. 'But you now feel you have no choice.'

'*We* have no choice.'

And just as his simple use of her name had rocked her as she received the weight of him, so too her use of 'we' leaves him staring at her with a look of … of, yes, gratitude. Gratitude for a kindness he thought never to receive. And, almost in a state of wonder, he reaches out and takes her hand. It is a thin hand, but warm. Life there, yet.

Together they leave the square, now all but emptied of trade, and walk down to the bridge and the stream and the fields beyond. Hand in hand. Like a middle-aged couple. And it occurs to her that this is how the town might see them. A contented middle-aged couple ambling, no particular destination in mind, through the town. And for the moment, she is content with that.

* * *

Do we enter these things knowingly? Or willingly? And do we really know what we set in motion when we do?

In the years that followed that meeting, Emily Hale had ample time to consider all of this. Emily Hale spends her days going back over her life, particularly those summers in England, unpicking the threads in the narrative, only to see the pattern reassemble itself; fate reassert itself. In a way, they were like those diplomats who, for the best and worst of motives, enter into murky negotiations to steer their countries through dangerous times. Secret negotiations were everywhere then. Every day, it seemed, the newspapers spoke of one set of talks or another, in towns or cities that were known, not known or soon became known because of the talks that took place in them, where grey-suited diplomats sat down to do their deals. But did these men ever really know, could they ever know, just what they were setting in motion? And did she and Tom?

For weren't they negotiating? Driven by motives both apparent and hidden or too late disclosed? And was it then, in those years between the wars, that she handed over her life, as diplomats handed over the sacrifice of small countries or duchies to gain concessions in the name of the greater good?

And did he accept it knowingly, in some murky part of his mind, while the rest of it looked the other way? Did she do likewise? Were they not negotiating, even if they never admitted as much?

Once I loved you as just anyone would, when I knew love at its purest. At its most unquestioning. Like faith. But the years took it from me, and now I have only the memory of those years when love like faith came easily: a young man on a spring morning. I had lost it, but through you I have recovered it. The memory of it. And although we can't have that kind of love again, for that kind of love comes only once, we can have *this*. We can be the keepers of that memory, and together we can preserve it. And be sustained by it. Love, pure. Untouchable. Never to be lost again. But only so long as it stays untouched. So long as we keep it out of the world's reach, for the world ruins everything. *These* are the loves that never rot because the contamination of the world can't infect them.

He never said any of this, not in so many words, that day or in any other of the days and talks between them that followed. No, they never said as much, but they understood each other or thought they did. This was the unspoken deal, was it not? Because the wreck, the human wreckage that fell into her arms that late afternoon by the town square, was capable of nothing more. And did she see this, did she know this in her bones even then, but choose not to look? Did she tell herself that this was a transitory state, one that would pass, and when it did they *would* become that contented middle-aged couple the town took them to be and bring their love down from the heavens and into the world?

And was there yet another part of the deal? For she knew what he meant by love withstanding the world, love that is immune to it. He meant Dante and Beatrice and all their kind, the doomed lovers that he kept in his coat pocket all those years before in a Boston garden. Lovers who pledge with their eyes, whose eyes kiss but whose lips never touch. Loves that, all the same, never fade, and never lower themselves into the world and the worldly, and never lose themselves in babble and silence, in accusation and indifference, care and violence, ardour and weariness. For if the pain and damage of past years was to mean anything for Tom, it had to have been for something more than just what the world calls love. It had to rise above all that, or the pain and the damage were all for nothing: meaningless pain and meaningless damage. It had to be immortal love. Was this the unspoken part of the deal? That it was not only her damaged Tom, the wreck, who needed her, but this other Tom too, this T.S. Eliot. And while her Tom talked of love like faith, was T.S. Eliot already at work? Was it as simple and complex and murky as that? Was that their marriage, after all? Give me my art and we will live on in the sanctuary of it. Forever. I will make our love immortal. Even though nothing of the sort was said, did they both enter into their pact knowingly?

Murky deals were everywhere then. It was an age of murky deals, and why shouldn't it include them? And was there not also a part of her that recognised that she liked it? Recognised that her vanity, the vanity that the upright Emily Hale rarely allowed to slip from her, was stirred. If she could not have the ordinary, human love she craved, she would have the consolation of *this*. She would, in the language of murky deals, 'settle' for this. Was there ever a precise moment when nods were exchanged? Or was it all so gradual they didn't notice? And did she suspect, even then, that all she would ever be left with would be the love letter, read by thousands through the centuries, and she the Lady of silences, the mute Beatrice in the background, who made it all possible. Did this stir the buried vanity of Emily Hale as surely as any worldly desire? For whenever she read those selected parts of his letters to her girls, was it not the vanity of Emily Hale that was being satisfied because no other part of her could be? Did she know all along, in her bones, that her reward for all the waiting was always going to come down to this: words in a book, Tom and Emily, two pale pressed flowers preserved forever between its pages? While all the time telling herself that their arrangement was a passing state, and that his delight could exist alone for only so long. For to abandon this hope would have left *only* vanity.

On one side the coastline — beaches, trees and holiday houses — slips by; on the other the vast expanse of the sea. Henry is concentrating at the wheel; the engine chugs, driving them on. A sailboat, come out from one of the beaches, nears, and the young vacation sailor waves. She waves back. It is a boat like Tom's. Small, but still big enough to take out into the sea and get into trouble. The satchel is still over her shoulder, shut and secure; the letters inside, old ink on old paper, the envelopes displaying small blue stamps with their images of dead kings, are still safely in her care.

She sways from side to side with the waves. Clouds swirl round above her, the sun is hidden one minute and bright the next, and there is an occasional rumbling in the sky. A storm is building, the sky will break. But not just yet. There is a groan from the clouds, the beast is impatient. She looks up, willing the clouds to burst, the sky to break and the beast to be released from an eternity of patient waiting.

PART TWO

An Extinct Order of Feeling

6.

Yes, deals were in the air. Murky, deceptive, driven by the best and the worst of intentions. All doomed. We wished for one thing, and History gave us another. Old lines gave way to new lines on maps in newspapers. The faraway names of faraway places became familiar. Life in that Cotswold town went on, more or less, in the same way: the same milkman in his horse-drawn cart, like a Roman charioteer; the same town gossips at the bus stop; the same bored young lovers making for the privacy of open fields. Timeless, but all of them running out of time.

The man in his sailboat has passed Eastern Point and disappeared into Gloucester Harbor, now far behind her. And Henry, saying nothing much, steers them on towards the waiting rocks. We talk of timeless places where time stands still, but only moments are timeless. Moments *in* time, but outside time. Moments that explode, like tiny atoms, into infinity. The tick-tock of everyday time raced on ahead of us that last summer and we gave up the chase, slowing down the way you do when something is ending and you are intent on taking in every second.

Emily is studying Henry. He looks ahead. Concentrating, absorbed in the task at hand, to the point, she imagines, that he does it without thinking. Of course he is thinking, but what? Occasional sea spray showers the deck. The sea calls, the land waves. The grey-blue sea becomes rolling fields. A country road winds into town. Limestone houses spring up around her. And then Tom is shaking a newspaper at her. Some new concession to the Führer. Another shady deal. Some new betrayal. As much as everything out there in the street went on the same way or seemed to, as much as everybody tried to go on the same way, it wasn't the same. Tom clenches the newspaper, white fury in his eyes.

'We are weak!' He speaks to her with a look of utter incomprehension. 'We don't even feel the shame in our humiliation.'

He throws the newspaper onto a table then strides to the window, looking out over the high street of the town. In the house opposite, a door opens; a familiar figure, a summer-time neighbour, ambles up the street. The storm passes, the fury eases, and he lets out a slow, helpless sigh. He doesn't turn, just frowns upon the spectacle of a town going about its business, oblivious of its humiliation. Beyond shame. Eventually, he speaks. And in a tone suggesting he can no longer bear to talk about politics, he changes the subject.

'It's a lovely town, but I don't like being dead. Not yet.'

He takes it personally, the weakness of the country. Treats it as a burden he took on with his citizenship. But she always wants to tell him: Tom, you'll never be one of them. She's watched him, time and again, playing at being an Englishman. Tipping his hat at the wrong time to the wrong people. Desperately trying to be one of them, but always getting it wrong. And she wants to tell him: Tom, you'll never get it right. You were never meant to. They won't let you. Don't you see it in their faces? When that bony Mrs Woolf looks at you and smiles, she's looking at a very fine counterfeit. Saying to herself, it's very good, isn't it? Tom, Tom, why don't you see it?

So Tom broods on the street, the white fury that possesses him from time to time, though calmed, still lurking. But as much as he was just full of fury and condemnation of the country, he still talks in terms of 'we'. 'We are weak,' he says, picking up where he left off, 'because we don't believe in anything. Heaven knows I loathe the communists, but at least they believe in something. We go to church and sing hymns. We recite Shakespeare,' he adds, with mounting passion, 'as *if* we read him. We talk of tradition, without having the faintest idea what it really is. It's just sounds. Mouths opening and closing. Empty words, the meaning of which everybody has long forgotten.' He shakes his head. 'More than weak, we are the walking dead and don't know it. And I don't want to be dead. Not even the walking dead. Not yet.'

He is speaking to her, and to no one. She doesn't answer, not because she agrees or doesn't agree, but because she has other things on her mind. All the same, she notes that these people who live easily with neither shame nor guilt are 'we', after all.

But just as he was seized with white fury, she is filled with fear. He is right: the town is carrying on as if nothing were happening. And time were not running out, as it is. This is how it happens. We assume there will always be a tomorrow and a tomorrow and that we have all the time in the world to fill in those tomorrows. When, in fact, time has sped up and we must slow down. For she is convinced that something immense is rolling towards them. And will soon be upon them. And with that conviction comes the unshakeable belief that this will be her last summer in the town. And it is all frightening because this immense event rolling towards them brings with it a terrible sense of finality.

And so Miss Emily Hale, at once in that lounge room and on the deck of the boat, resolved to slow down that day, to slow time. She resolved to make plans, when all about her nobody was making any. And she decided to confront that terrible imminence with her plans.

* * *

'I don't like being dead either. Or never having lived. Is there any difference?'

They are out on the high street and she asks this question as if he knows about these things, having lived more than she has. And although, to an extent, he will always be her Boston

Tom, ungrounded and still not quite grown up, who knows no more about these things than she does, although that memory of him persists, she is also aware of the fact – plainly written in his haunted face – that he does. At least, knows about a certain kind of living, knowledge of which she wants too. The knowledge of what passes between couples in the night. What heaven or what hell. She is forty-eight and has never known what it is to hear someone breathing beside her in the night. Never felt the twitches or heard the murmurs of someone dreaming beside her and never been given cause to wonder what they might be dreaming. All this, and so much more. And as much as she might wear his ring – not on her wedding finger – she has only the ring, not the knowledge that ought to come with it. All the same, this imminence is upon them, and Emily Hale is making plans.

They walk past a bookshop and Emily stops, gazing in. Tom, unaware, continues on along the high street. Then realising he is talking to himself, he turns round and sees Emily, who beckons him back.

'Look,' she says, smiling and pointing at something in the window.

As he follows her finger, he sees it. Or, rather, them. Two books side by side. In the centre of the window: *The Symbolist Movement in Literature*, by Arthur Symons, and *Prufrock and Other Observations*, by T.S. Eliot.

They are both silent. Tom, ever so slowly, is shaking his head from side to side, as if wondering who on earth that young man was who stumbled across the right book at the right moment all those years ago. Reliving the thrill of that morning when *anything* seemed possible, and remembering that this is how it was, how it is: that art, like life, begins in wonder. And that it is so easy to lose that sense of wonder. Or have it pounded out of you.

Emily looks at Tom. Is he, for the moment, young again: strong with the strength of youth, not broken, registering the spell of old magic? Maybe. For there is wonder in his eyes.

For Emily, it will always be a puzzle. She's never thought much of the book itself. But she understands it is just the kind of book to open doors for a young man, just so long as you're young, with the wonder still in you, when you read it. Not such a good book, but the right book at the right time, all the same.

In unison, as if thinking the same thought at the same moment – 'Enough of this' – they turn, their movements almost appearing choreographed, and continue their walk along the high street. Half-familiar faces pass them in the street. They greet them. Tom and Emily are, indeed, what the town takes to be a middle-aged couple, out on a morning walk.

'There *is*,' she says.

'Is what?'

'A difference. Never having lived is a kind of death-in-life. I'd rather endure hell than that – at least you'd know you're alive.'

He sighs, as if to say, would you? Would you *really*? 'What has brought this on?'

She takes his hand. He takes hers. They are holding on to each other. '*This* has brought this on.' She gestures towards the sky, the town, the day. 'It's all going to change. And it's no use us going on as if we've all the time in the world and I'll be back next summer. And everything will go on and on as it always has. Because it won't. I won't be back. At least, I fear I won't.'

'And I fear you're right.'

Then, lifting both their hands to the sky, she plunges in. 'Let's get away, Tom. There's always somebody around. My aunt, my uncle, somebody dropping in. Oh, they mean well, but there's always someone. Let's just drive off some place for the day. Wouldn't that be fun?'

They move on a couple of paces and come to a stop at the marketplace noticeboard. The summer pantomime, a pageant of sorts, is being performed that night by an oddly democratic – or is it just medieval – collection of locals, from nobles to farm hands. They have tickets. Everybody is expected to be there – on the lawns of an estate just a few minutes walk from the town.

'It's a sort of slapstick Shakespeare,' she says, and he smiles as they walk on.

She takes heart from that. Her Tom is in that smile. Young Tom. That much of him has survived from the wreckage. And so, taking heart, she names a town.

'That would be nice, don't you think? A whole day. To ourselves.'

He nods: yes, that would be nice. Emily watches as Thacher

Island looms and Henry peers into the distance. Oh, the simplest things mattered then. There they were; there they are. Once again she takes his hand, and they move on. A middle-aged couple setting out on their morning walk as they do every morning, making plans.

7.

At some point her top slipped, exposing her shoulder as well as the mark. She didn't notice when; they were too busy drawing on the rolled cigarette mixed with dope. Just a cigarette, she kept telling herself. Nothing to it. What's the fuss? Now it is finished and she looks down at her exposed shoulder, wondering when that happened but making no attempt to pull the top back into place. She has, she tells herself, just smoked a joint. For the first time. What's the fuss, she thought. Just a cigarette. But then she stopped talking and everything slowed down and went strangely quiet. A bird took forever to cross the sky. The time on her watch never seemed to change. And now she can feel herself slipping into a dreamy state. Into a dream world. Just like Alice. And if someone, one of her friends back in New York, were to ask her what it's like, she knows what she'd say: go ask Alice.

Grace and Ted are sitting in the front seat of his car on the outskirts of the town, looking out over the peaceful summer countryside. And she's not sure if the countryside looks dreamy because she's gone all dreamy, or because it is. The trees seem to hum in the breeze, the leaves shimmer. They took their time, taking turns to draw on the joint, watching it slowly turn to ash, then leaned back, saying nothing, as it slowly delivered them into a wonderland that really did leave her feeling as though she could talk to the trees. Not in words, not everyday words, at least, but the way you talk in dreams. Why not? Everything seems possible. And at some point her top, thin, creamy cotton, slipped over her shoulder. She looks down at the mark, studying it as though she's never looked at it before, not really. Then she looks up at Ted. She makes no attempt to pull the top back. It is her sign to him, and she invites him to her with her eyes. And as his lips fall on her neck she is aware of lips and skin and touch in a way she never has before. Ted, with the dark eyes of a poet, except he's never written a line and never will; Grace, with the blue eyes of a dreamy Alice. Blue meets black. Then she feels his teeth, biting into her neck. Vampiric. A bit of an animal. And her dreaminess dissolves for a moment as she pulls his head back.

'No. Miss Hale wouldn't like it.' Then she pauses and corrects herself with a smile. 'No, Miss Hale would love it. If she'd only let herself.'

This he takes as an invitation and leans his head forward again, only to be stopped again.

'No,' she says, 'one mark is enough. God, I'm being branded!' She bursts out laughing. And it's as though she's hearing her own laughter for the first time. And *everything* is like this. So, she slowly nods to herself, this is what the fuss is about.

He slumps back in the seat, looking out over the green countryside. Grace does likewise. She's had a thought. Hazy, but there. A thought, all right. At the mention of Miss Hale she pictured her lounge room. The room in which they sit for her lessons: the furniture old like the cottage; the paintings on the walls; and the framed snaps on the sideboard. Above all, she's remembering the mirror reflection of Miss Hale in her study, pulling out a drawer of her desk and slipping the notes in, before she forgets, no doubt, and goes leaving money lying all around the house.

All the way out here Ted was talking about the guitar in the music-shop window. And now, slumped in the driver's seat, he's telling her again he was destined for that guitar. It was destined for him. And she can see it, except she doesn't tell him that he's living yesterday's dream. It's late July, not long and the trees will take on that tinted autumn glow, and she'll be gone. And their lives afterwards will be lived as though on different planets, not just in different cities. And not for the first time, she's convinced she's looking at the best of Ted. No, life won't give him much. But she can do something for Ted. She can give him something that life won't: the guitar.

Her casual remark about money, and how it always turns up, comes back to her. Miss Hale slips the notes into the drawer of her desk then closes it. She has other students: her 'girls', she calls them. And if Grace's money goes into that drawer, why not theirs? Could be quite a bit there. Old ladies stash money all over their houses. It's a hazy thought, hazy like the late-morning countryside out there. Miss Hale won't miss it, she tells herself with a casualness that surprises her. It all seems very clear, really. And right. All in a good cause. A little something for Ted. Making up for life's oversights.

And with the same dreamy casualness with which her thoughts unfolded, she tells Ted all about it.

'I know where Miss Hale puts her money.'

Ted looks at her, as if just having woken up.

'What money?'

'For the lessons. Not just mine, but all her girls'.'

'What are you saying?'

'Money, I told you. It always turns up.'

Ted turns from her, back to the countryside, and then back to Grace. And she knows exactly what he's thinking, because she's thinking it too. At the same time, she can't believe she's telling him this. And with a dreamy casualness that makes it all sound so logical. So reasonable. For all her old Boston ways and occasional bursts of impatience, or whatever it is that bursts out of her every now and then, and as much as she'd like to shake the Henry James thing right out of her, she likes Miss Hale. Has come to feel that they have a sort of bond. And she shouldn't really be telling Ted or anybody about this. But she's all dreamy like Alice and telling herself that Miss Hale won't miss it. It's just a little extra cash that she doesn't notice, not really. But Ted will.

'Every Wednesday night she goes to a church meeting. She told me.'

'That's tonight,' he says, trance-like.

'Yeah,' she says, a long, drawn-out, puzzled yeah, as if she's wondering who on earth is talking.

'What time?'

'Not sure. Night.'

They both sit perfectly still for a minute, possibly two, neither saying anything. She looks down at her shoulder, rubs the mark that Ted left, and makes no attempt to pull the top back up. It's her sign to him. Her offering. Her neck. That's the other thing about her Ted phase: the fucking. She'd fucked before she came here. All the girls at her school started fucking early. It was just something you did. So she knew what a fuck was. But Ted knew a few things too. Things that she didn't. And now she's about to fuck stoned. For the first time. Like fucking for the first time. She's dreamy, he's dreamy. Her top has slipped. She leaves it. It is her sign.

The drive into town, an hour or so later, is slow. The dope is beginning to wear off, and already she's beginning to wonder just what she's said and what she might have set in motion. At the same time she's telling herself it's just like one of those bright ideas you get at three in the morning and forget about by breakfast. She says nothing more about it, Ted says nothing more. He'll forget. They'll forget. They were both pretty dreamy. Just like Alice.

8.

A small boy runs across the lawn of a country estate, arms outstretched like the wings of an aeroplane coming in to land. In one hand he clutches a single sheet of paper. He has flown in from the darkness at the edge of the gardens and lands in the glare of a spotlight. He folds his wings and raises his arm, brandishing the sheet of paper.

'Out of this nettle Danger ...' he proclaims confidently, then trails into uncertainty. 'We ...' There is a pause and mumbling from the bushes behind him. 'We pluck this flower Safety.'

The audience gathered on the lawns breaks into loud applause; a woman calls out to her neighbour, 'That's Mr Chamberlain.' His job done, the prologue complete, the boy withdraws and a warrior king enters, standing at the centre of the garden stage, sword in hand.

All through the twilight and into the early evening, the town's population has been assembling on the estate lawns for the annual summer pantomime, only this year they're calling it a pageant. There is a line of motor cars in the driveway – Rolls-Royces, Bentleys and nippy little sports cars – the chauffeurs leaning against their vehicles and smoking in the moonlight;

the sound of applause now and then coming to them on a light summer breeze.

Emily and Tom are sitting on fold-out garden chairs, Emily's aunt and uncle beside her. She is watching Tom as much as the performance, her mood dependent on his responses. From the start his expression is a mixture of pained resignation and amusement, through a succession of warrior kings, dreamy kings, young women driven mad by love and sickly youths driven mad by ghosts. An actor asks the audience at one point what it all means and what are we all doing here, only to hear the audience respond in robust voice that they thought the actor might tell *them*. It is an exchange that brings a smile to Tom's face. But it is only when the town smith appears, wearing a daisy-chain crown, Lear in exile, accompanied by the lad the town calls simple, Eric playing the Fool – and all will agree later, after the show, playing the part to perfection – that Tom lets out a long, booming laugh: the sort of booming laugh that turns heads, as it does right now, and which speaks of the warm heart that she knows is there beneath the cold reserve he presents to the world. The booming laugh that speaks of the impish humour and the prankster's sense of fun that she well remembers from their early days before he left for this old world, at once old and dangerous, and from which she would dearly love to pluck him, like the flower from the nettle. They'll never let you in, Tom. You will never be one of them. Come home. The booming laugh dies down, the smile stays. And as the show progresses, she becomes more and more involved in the constantly changing cardboard sets, as an astonishing range of potted plays passes from one side of the lawns, each to enjoy its few minutes in the spotlight, to the other side, and back into darkness.

And then a young woman appears onstage alone, Juliet leaning on an invisible balcony, appealing to her Romeo. She is just a lone young woman on a bare, open lawn, but she creates the whole of Verona around her, and Emily can't understand how she's doing it. Furthermore, she's familiar, this young woman. But how? From when? And where? And then she realises that this is the young woman, Catherine, whose name she's never forgotten, who cleaned their cottages that first summer and autumn that Emily came to the town. The same young woman who was forever in the company of a young man from the town. She is older now, but it's her. And it is only after Emily has remembered all of this that she realises that the lawns, the gardens and the entire gathered audience have fallen into silence. The buffoonery has gone out of the night. This young woman stands on a bare, open lawn and creates Verona from nothing, the audience hanging on her every gesture and word as she addresses her Romeo. And once again, Emily asks herself how she does this. Emily Hale, the born actor who has played this role in school productions but was never allowed to set foot on a professional stage. She comes to the obvious and only conclusion – that this young woman does it by acting. She has silenced the mob. She has stilled them. She has the gift. And as she concludes this she turns to Tom who is as silent as everyone else. And what she discerns is the rapt look she noticed all those years before in the parlour of his cousin's house when she sang of dreaming waves and lone delight. She wonders if he too is thinking of this. And then, with a final invocation of sweet tomorrows, the young woman passes in liquid steps from the spotlighted lawn to the darkness of the gardens. For a moment, the ground that she occupied is empty in a way that it hasn't been all night. The silence lingers, then breaks, as the audience, transformed by the spectacle of a lone young woman whose magic tricks gave them all a private Verona in which to dwell for a few minutes, bursts into prolonged, explosive applause that turns the heads and raises the eyebrows of the chauffeurs gathered at their Rolls-Royces and Bentleys in the driveway outside.

And with the applause Emily becomes aware of Tom's hand enfolding hers, and she can't be sure how long it's been there. Did they, indeed, think the same thoughts without need of speaking? Amid the buffoonery and laughter of the performance, did they actually rediscover one of those moments that survives, and which, together with all other such moments, forms a golden thread back through the years to where it all began in that Boston parlour?

A tumbling row of touchingly inept acrobats passes across the lawns, and then a drenched figure, seemingly crawling from a shipwreck, asks, 'What place is this?' – and the audience responds, calling out the name of the town. So the night goes: burlesque succeeded by pantomime, succeeded by vaudeville – until the show is over and the boy who performed the prologue comes weaving in across the lawns to land, and standing before the audience bids them all goodnight, holding a single flower aloft.

Then the entire cast spills onto the lawn: barbers, butchers, the odd young aristocrat and the odd young lady, farmers, labourers, milkmen, barmaids, teachers, estate agents – all one for the night, before filing back into town and reassuming their assigned ranks and roles. And somewhere among them, the young woman who gave them all a private Verona to dwell in for a few minutes. Although with so many up there on the lawn, under a spotlight borrowed from someone who knew someone in the movies, it is, Emily decides, impossible to pick her.

Emily's aunt and uncle have gone, and Emily and Tom stroll back into the town across an open field with the rest of the audience. There is enough moonlight to see that there is contentment on his face.

'I've packed a hamper.'

'Cheese?' he asks.

She nods, he smiles.

'What was your favourite bit?'

He whispers in her ear. 'The Fool.'

She laughs. 'Played his part to perfection.'

And it is here that he lets out that booming laugh again, and as he does, heads turn all around them, looking for the source of such unbound laughter, smiling as they turn.

And so, one of the crowd, but not one of the crowd, side by side, presenting to the world the image of a late middle-aged couple, they stroll back into town amid a gathering chorus of popular singalongs: of blackbirds, and red, red robins and blue skies.

* * *

'You drive real fine, ma'am. Yes, that's for sure. You're a real fine driver.'

The air hits their faces, fanning Tom's hair back, blasting away the carefully combed part that, over the years, has shifted from the middle to the side of his head. They are travelling in a borrowed open car. Emily is at the wheel; Tom, it is generally thought, an uncertain driver. They are rushing along a deep country lane towards a town not so far away, but far enough to feel as though they have created a space of their own: to feel like they are getting away. A pretty town, on a canal.

'And you, Mr Eliot, you're from St Louis? St *Louis*? And there I was thinking you were an Englishman. In that tweed coat and tweed pants and that tweed cap of yours, you look *so* English.'

The sun, directly above them, is bright – but there are troubling dark clouds just above the rolling hills in front of them. She eyes them, and presses a little harder on the accelerator. They have been talking to each other in this way for most of the drive. Not so much talking as calling out over the rush of the air and the sound of the engine. This is the Tom she remembers. The playful Tom. The Boston Tom, who loved accents — especially the sound of his lost midwestern accent — the Tom who went away and never really came back. Except for moments like this, when he could be the old Tom in his cousin's garden. The young Tom. Her Tom. But of course, he's not. There will only ever now be flashes of that Tom.

The deep laneway rushes up to meet them with alarming speed as he calls out to Emily.

'You know, ma'am, you sure drive real good. But has anybody ever told you, Miss Hale, you've got one helluva lead foot?'

'You mean to tell me, Mr Eliot, that a Missouri man is frightened of a little speed?'

'Not frightened, Miss Hale — only cows frighten me; don't have many cows in my part of Missouri. No, Miss Hale, not frightened. Just puzzled. You're a very careful lady. Why, you're careful about what you say and how you say it, careful about being on time and only smoking in the evenings — and no more than two cocktails. And so refined in what you read. Don't get me wrong: I'm a Missouri man, I love my books — give me a good western any day — but put you behind the wheel of a car and something happens.'

She smiles at him as he shifts his gaze from her to the laneway, betraying a hint of alarm. But only a hint. For in all the summers she's been coming here, she's never seen him so relaxed. So young. Perhaps it's Time the healer doing that.

Perhaps it's because she's going back, and will not, they both realise, be coming here again for some time. Possibly years. And isn't that always the way? You never really care for someone or love them as much as when they're leaving you and you're leaving them. The way the lighthouse bids farewell to the boat, and the way the sailor eyes the lighthouse and the harbour with sad longing, before turning to the open sea.

'And you're wondering, Mr Eliot, what other surprises I've got in me?' She winks.

He laughs, a resounding laugh that is quickly lost in the wind. 'I sure am, Miss Hale. I sure am.'

'You ever met a Boston lady before, Mr Eliot?'

'Why, no, ma'am. Boston ladies are as scarce as cows in Missouri.'

'No cows in Missouri?'

'Not in my part, ma'am.'

'You're *sure* you're from Missouri? You look *so* English.'

'Sure as I can be about anything.'

'And you've never met a Boston lady before? Well, let me teach you a few things about Boston ladies.'

'You already have, ma'am. You already have.'

The clouds above the rolling hills are gathering. Dark clouds. She doesn't like the look of them and wishes them away. But she knows they're not going anywhere. And they are driving right towards them. The game pauses, and she concentrates on the laneway in front of them, with (clouds aside) a light heart and a heavy foot. He, still betraying a hint of alarm at the speed with which the lane meets them, raises his head to the diminishing blue sky above the shaded lane.

They continue, the wind notwithstanding, in relative silence. The lane opening out into villages, then closing in again; Tom and Emily occasionally stopping at this village and that, tempted by country markets and tea houses, before continuing on their way.

By mid-afternoon they arrive at a large village, and pull up at an inn beside the mill. With the wind no longer fanning their faces and the engine off, a dreamy silence falls on them. There is a stream, and it really is silver in the sunlight. And ducks, and reeds. A young boy fishes from the bank, and a flock of sheep crosses the small stone bridge that fords the stream.

She looks at him, a theatrical arching of the eyebrow. 'I hope you appreciate the view, Mr Eliot; it took quite a bit of organising.'

'I do, Miss Hale. You Boston ladies sure know how to organise a man.'

'Man, nature and beasts, Mr Eliot,' she adds, then frowns as she scans the view. 'I ordered a hay-wain.'

She sits back in the driver's seat, removing her shiny leather gloves. He lights a cigarette, one of his French things, and she notes straight away that the air is filled with the smell of a crowded French café.

'Well,' he says in his normal voice and drawing on the cigarette, 'there are fields out there. Shall we stroll across them or stride?'

'Let's amble.'

'Amble?' he asks, looking at the rolling dark clouds closing in over the rolling green hills. 'What about the clouds?'

'What clouds? Don't tell me a Missouri man is afraid of a little water.'

And so, already dressed in walking clothes, they gather the hamper and a rug from the back of the car, and with no destination in mind cross the small stone bridge, recently vacated by the sheep. But before they even reach the other side, a spear of lightning flashes across the sky, followed by a crack of thunder that almost rocks the bridge beneath them.

* * *

The crump of thunder, like distant bombing, turns her head. Henry is unmoved. Or so it seems. As they pass between Thacher Island and the holiday beaches of the coastline, they come into view: the Dry Salvages. Henry turns from the wheel and nods in their direction. It is the first time she has ever looked at them from the sea, in a boat. And the view transforms them. Although some distance away – possibly two or three miles, it's hard to judge – they possess a sense of immanence and danger they don't have when viewed from the land. And a sense of possession, for they also now assume a manner that says, you're in *my* world. Salvages. *Les Trois Sauvages.* Savages. If that's right, if that's the derivation – and nobody really knows – but if that's right she can understand why the early sailors and fishermen would have called them that. For they possess an unmoveable, unshakeable sense of always having been here. A sound like a roar or a deep moan, the very sound of the rocks themselves, carries over the water towards them. We came before you, they say, and we will be here after you. Yes, they have this air of having seen it all. You come, you go, these rocks say, but we remain. You're in my watery world now. And I am neither god nor lord nor chief. I simply am. Before you, and after you.

A creeping sense of apprehension, which she hadn't anticipated, possesses her. And with it, a foreboding. As if some great event were about to happen and she were merely meeting her destiny. Like those nights that give every impression of already having happened, and will again. As though the twain, long in converging, were about to close in on itself, and the two of them, the rocks and Emily, had always been sailing towards this moment. Except she's only just realised. Impulsively, she slips her shoes off and stands barefoot on the deck, drawn to the rocks with a secret longing. Mesmerised. She steps forward and grips the railing. You rocks! You granite shores! You have waited all this time. Such patience. I am here, I have come. And I am no stranger to you, for you know me as surely as I know you.

And they are exactly as Tom described them. Teeth. Giant granite teeth. Looking, in calm seas, harmless enough. But not today. Waves wash over them, momentarily concealing the threat, then withdraw, the sea once again baring its teeth. The primeval groan calling to her over the water. Back and forth, back and forth. Now hidden, now revealed.

Even from this distance she is in their thrall. There is another crack of thunder as the storm clouds that have threatened to break all day roll round in the sky; the summer sun, like the rocks, now hidden, now bright and high above her. She calls out to Henry, concentrating on the way ahead.

'How close can we get?'

He turns to her. Puzzled, concerned. Possibly alarmed. Yes, definitely alarmed. She sees all of this in his expression. A man asking himself what has he got himself into? She stands with her bag over her shoulder that no one is allowed to touch, just as she herself can barely endure being touched. And she's jumpy, has been all morning. Difficult. Yes, that's what he sees. A difficult, jumpy woman. And becoming more difficult by the minute. He wouldn't be the first to call her difficult. The whole town, she imagines, does. There goes Emily Hale. Spent all her life waiting for Mr Eliot. And he promised her this, he promised her that ... when the time was right. When the time ... But the time was never right. And then he up and married again. Not telling anyone. Up and married his secretary, thirty-eight years younger. And Miss Hale went mad. Miss Hale went to hospital. Miss Hale never really recovered. And then Mr Eliot died. And she not only had nothing left to wait for, but nothing at all. Just days that she didn't know what to do with. Too many of them. There goes Miss Hale. That's what the town sees. That's what Henry sees. A difficult woman. Broken Miss Hale, asking how close they can get to the rocks. Not just asking, demanding to know. And her shoes, where have her shoes gone? For she's standing barefoot on the deck and she wasn't a moment before. It's all in his expression – that and the question of just what has he got himself into and why didn't he see it coming?

He looks back to Thacher Island, turns to the sky and the rolling clouds, shakes his head and calls out, 'We've seen enough.'

'No!'

It is shrill. The shrill cry of a desperate woman who, having lived a life of denial, will *not* now be denied. 'Take me to them. Take me ...'

More than this refusal to be denied, she radiates the distinct impression that she might do anything. And at this very moment, she just might. With one hand she clutches the railing, with the other the satchel. Then she pushes herself off the railing and walks back barefoot to the middle of the deck, now wet from sea spray and the occasional wave, and looks directly ahead at the rocks. And taking her hand off the satchel, she raises her arm as if greeting them, the way you would greet someone in the street. I'm here. I've come. At last!

* * *

The thunder dies. The dark clouds roll in over the green hills. They leave the small stone bridge behind them and amble out into the fields. But it is more of a studied amble than a natural one. For no matter how much they may choose to ignore the sky, they know it is only a matter of time (and not much at that) before it falls on them.

He smooths the rug in a patch of sun, and they lounge, the hamper basket open, as if posing for a portrait on a perfect summer's day. But it is, if anything, a studied portrait in ignoring the inevitable. Within minutes, the first drops of rain fall. Big drops. They don't so much fall as thud into the rug, onto the basket and onto them. Lightning spears the sky, thunder fills the air. The drops, falling like molten lead, are gathering and the sky is minutes from opening. They rise quickly, collect everything, the basket only half fastened, and make a dash for the stone bridge they ambled over only a short time before, the inn beckoning on the other side of the stream. The sun is gone from the sky, black swirling clouds have claimed it entirely, and night is falling in mid-afternoon.

When they reach the bridge they both see, with bleak resignation, that the car (a borrowed one) is uncovered. They throw the basket into the back and draw the cover over the car. By the time they secure it, the rain is heavy, and when, seconds later, they reach the inn, it is a deluge. Tom looks at her, a pleased smile on his face as though everything, the whole day, has gone perfectly to plan.

'Heavens,' he says, 'we'll need an ark.'

They are wet, but not drenched. Seconds later and they would have been. It is that kind of downpour. And rather than go straight inside, they stand in the shelter of the doorway, mesmerised by the spectacle, for it is magnificent. The landscape is transformed. The heavens have fallen on them. Emphatically. A demonstration of what they can do. Look upon my works ... And to Emily (and she can see the same sentiment in Tom's face as he looks upon heaven's works), there is something wonderfully cleansing about the whole thing. As though all the tired make-believe of a make-believe summer, the dead traditions and the shame and humiliation of all the grubby deals of a grubby age were being washed away, and something mighty were revealing itself and reminding them that they are one with rocks, trees and birds, and that like the birds, wheeling in the sky for the safety of boughs and branches, they are only here for a short while.

But as they stand in silent awe, they see, and with increasing disquiet, that the deep lane they drove on into the village is already going under. That the deluge, if anything, is intensifying, and that the lane and the road through the village will soon be flooded. The stream too is rising, and the ducks have evacuated to its diminishing banks. The rain is not so much falling any more as pouring down upon them. And the afternoon sky, midnight black, shows no sign of becoming lighter. No, this is no summer downpour that will dump on them, quickly exhaust itself, then roll away, leaving the sun to re-emerge and summer to reassert itself after being rudely interrupted. No, the clouds, thick and black, stretch out to the very horizon.

Inside, they order drinks and food, having been denied their picnic. And as they look out the window over the next hour or so, their elation begins to fade. When a middle-aged woman comes to clear the plates, she notes the covered car at the front of the inn.

'Is that yours?'

Emily looks up and nods.

'It won't do you much good today.'

Emily smiles. 'We were just saying we'll need an ark out there.'

Without looking up, the woman says, 'We don't run to arks. Mind you, I wouldn't take one out in that even if we did. You'll be needing a room.'

Tom and Emily look at each other, neither, clearly, having thought of this.

The woman continues. 'And you're in luck. We've one left. But only one; you're not the only couple stranded here.'

'It's got to ease sometime, surely,' Emily says.

'Just look, missus. It's not going to ease, and the roads are flooded. You're stuck. And I'd take that room before someone else does.'

But Emily only hears part of this. *Missus.* She called her missus. So naturally, as if there were no doubt in the world that they really were the middle-aged couple that the town takes them for. As though, over the years, they have become what they seem.

She looks at Tom, an expression on her face that says: what shall we do, what *can* we do? In tandem they turn and look out the window, then turn back to each other. He raises his eyebrows, surrendering to the inevitable. She nods and looks up at the woman. 'We'll take it.'

Within minutes they are standing at the desk.

'What name?' the woman says.

'Eliot,' Emily says. One *l*.'

'Mr and Mrs Eliot, then,' the woman says, looking up and smiling. 'Room three.'

The woman leads them up the stairs, and opens the door onto a room that on another day would be bright with sunshine. For the window looks out onto the stream and the bridge and the fields beyond. But it's not the view that Tom and Emily are struck by. It is the bed. For there it is, the first thing you see upon entering the room. A large, imposing double bed that seems to take up half the space. And neither Tom nor Emily can take their eyes off it.

'Is there a problem?' the woman asks. 'It's our best room, I think. And besides, all the others are taken.'

They turn from the bed that sits there like some smug rake, leering at them as if to say, oh, come on, I'm just a bed. A big, bouncy bed, and I'm all yours, Mr and Mrs Eliot.

Emily is the first to recover.

'No, there's no problem. It's a nice room.'

'Good,' the woman says. 'There's a basin there. And the necessary is just down the hall. There's an umbrella downstairs, to get your things from the car when there's a chance.' And here she turns to Tom, smiling. 'I suspect that might be a job for Mr Eliot.'

She then holds up the key and says, 'Now, who shall I give this to?'

And as the question is directed at Emily, she reaches for it. 'I'll take that.'

The woman excuses herself, closes the door behind her, and suddenly, dramatically, with the click of the door, Tom and Emily are alone. Mr and Mrs Eliot. In the one room. *Their* room. And the prospect of the whole night before them.

* * *

When they have inspected the room and drawn the curtains back fully to catch the most of what light there is, she drops onto the bed and he into an armchair. The puzzle of how to go about this thing still hanging unspoken in the air.

Later, after wandering around the inn – and there's not much of it, except for a small reading room with out-of-date newspapers and antique magazines – and after a meal of cold meat and beer (Emily has discovered that, like Tom, she has found a taste for the local beer), and exchanging short greetings with the other guests – a young couple and a traveller – they return to their room and the unresolved question of how to go about this.

Emily looks out the window, and the rain pouring down the glass.

'Who'd have thought it?' she laughs. 'The flood.'

Then, in a no-nonsense manner, as if to suggest this is all very simple, she places his pillow at the foot of the bed. There. Emily at one end of the bed, Tom at the other. Simple. Yes? Tom nods, smiles with a slight, consenting lift of the shoulders, and is tempted, no doubt, to add in midwestern tones that Miss Hale sure knows how to organise a man, but resists. And while Emily feels a little like the sergeant major that she's sure Mrs Woolf thinks she is, there is also a certain approval in Tom's look. She has done well.

She turns back to the window, shaking her head. 'Have you ever seen such rain? That little stream will be a river now.'

'A river?' And this time he does drop into his midwestern accent. 'I've swum in the Mississippi, Miss Hale. Now, that's a river. And we don't just have storms, we have cyclones. You're thankful if your roof doesn't blow away in the night.'

She passes up the invitation to join the game and smiles. '*We*, you just said *we*.'

He smiles back, raises his eyebrows in agreement and sits on the bed; she joins him. 'So I did,' he says, with a kind of puzzled wonder, as if to say, where did that come from? 'So I did.'

She studies him: serious Tom, middle-aged Tom, contemplative Tom. More like those portraits of him that you sometimes see in bookshops and inside the books themselves than ever before. 'It catches me by surprise, every time. Heaven only knows what sparks it. But I can be standing in Russell Square, and suddenly I'm in the boat, my old catboat, in Gloucester. *Happy.* Impossibly so. I can smell the air and the sea. Feel the gentle rocking of the waves. See the wide blue sky – and it's always blue. And wide. Then I'm back in Russell Square again. I've got a pile of manuscripts to read, letters of polite rejection to write and a meeting to prepare for in a smoky room. And I ask myself how I ended up here, when all the time I know.'

He looks down at the floor, pausing between thoughts, and she lets him be. 'And sometimes when I see myself back there ...'

'Home?'

He shrugs. 'Perhaps.'

'What do you see?'

He pauses for a moment, the puzzled look still on his face, as if gazing into the heart of an enigma. 'Another life, altogether. A university lecturer who dabbles in poetry in his spare time. Writes poems that he keeps in a drawer. And never shows anyone. But happy. Perhaps, even, Professor Eliot. It's what my mother and father wanted. Instead,' he says, shaking his head, seemingly mystified by the form his life has taken, 'I chose the mug's game.'

And it is then that the Tom who became T.S. Eliot – the T.S. Eliot who looks down from bookshop walls, the famous public figure, god-like and all-knowing, infinitely patient, as if about to begin a lecture on some complex matter in a manner that suggests: this is difficult, but I'll explain it in a way that you will understand – it is then that he says to her, with utter conviction and no pretence (for there can be none in this room, sitting on this bed with the incessant rain beating on the window), that he can't help but feel he has made a complete mess of his life. That he has, over the years, come to look upon his life the way his father did. Or would have. A mess, a shambles. All of it, everything, a waste. Of time, of energy. Of a *life*! All of it – the thing that people call fame, the applause of strangers, the approval of fools, the stories reported to him of college students casually throwing lines from his poems into conversations as if their remembering the lines in itself were wit – all of it is a mug's game. He glances at her, a faraway look in his eyes. 'When I imagine myself back in Gloucester, I remember *exactly* how it was. Untying the moorings and setting out. Especially that feeling of setting out. The sun just up. The air fresh. And nobody about. Everything new. And exciting. The air sharp. The crack of the sail in the wind, the smell of the paint. But what I remember, above all, is being *happy*. I remember how happiness came easily then. So easily, I took it for granted. Then I'm back in Russell Square: manuscripts and meetings and stale rooms.'

There is much that she could say, for he is silent now. All the usual things, all the usual consolations you could say. All the talk of achievements, of having done something with your life. Which is both true and not true. And which matters and doesn't matter, depending on the moment. But she gauges the moment for such talk is wrong. He doesn't want to hear it. She's not sure he wants to hear anything. Besides, there is a strong part of her that agrees with everything he's been saying. That he has made a mess of his life, that he has paid too dearly for it, and that her suspicion, formed all those years ago in his cousin's garden, has been confirmed by the years: that there was something erratic and ungrounded in Tom Eliot, a hairline crack in the golden bowl, a flaw in the crystal; that for all his Boston manners, his properness, punctiliousness and considered air, Tom Eliot did not come with a guarantee. None of which she could possibly say. Just as he rarely mentions the impulsive, the reckless marriage that was at the heart of the mess of his life and still is. But then, he doesn't have to. Everybody knows. And yet, for all that, for some years now she's told herself that everyone is allowed to make a mistake once, and has resolved to do all she can to rescue Tom Eliot from the wreckage.

And so, deciding to leave all of the things she could say for another time, she simply takes his hand, the hint of a smile in her eyes. 'Don't ever forget, Mr Eliot, like the man says: you've come a long way from St Louis.'

'But baby,' he intones solemnly, as if reciting Dante, 'I still got a long way to go.'

She returns the solemn look, but with the hint of a smile. The Boston Tom, she thinks. He's still there, if you wave the right wand.

'Did you really swim in the Mississippi?'

He leans his head back and laughs, a laugh, she notes, that has a bit of a boom in it. And she'd like to think she put the boom there.

'Of course not,' he says, his laughter dying down. 'Some fools do. Not me. Have you ever seen the Mississippi?'

She shakes her head.

'It's brown, it's a mile wide. Currents swirl like snakes. In another age, people would have worshipped it as you worship a god and bathed on its banks.'

The light is back in his eyes. His laugh is back. He might even be happy. It is dark. She stands and kisses his forehead, a blessing before bed. She walks round to her side of the bed. He takes his shoes off. He loosens his tie as his head sinks into his pillow. She removes her earrings, places them on the bedside table and leans back, his feet beside her, hers beside him. And as she reaches out for the bedside lamp, she pauses, then quietly intones the words she's waited all her life to say. 'Goodnight, Tom.'

And, as he replies, she switches the lamp off and the room falls into darkness. The rain still beating on the window.

* * *

At some point, and she's not sure what time it is, she wakes. And she's not sure why she has woken. Then she realises that it is the silence, and the moonlight coming in through the window. For the rain has stopped, and out there in the night the clouds have parted. And on the other side of the bed she can hear the regular breathing of Tom in a deep sleep, and see his chest rising and falling with every breath. The heavy breathing of a lifetime smoker. All those French cigarettes. Breath, in and out. Tom's. He is *there*. Close enough to touch.

The young of this young world. The young … the young … The salty sea air blows on Emily's face. The boat rises and falls with the swell and the waves. Oh, the young today have no idea what it was like. To lie there, close enough to touch and not touch. To watch lips part and breathe and close and not kiss. To observe the folded hands that would touch and not hold them. But it was exquisite. Sublime. A communion you can't even conceive of, for the sensibility that made it possible has gone. One age *feels* differently from another age. No, you will never understand what it was like to lie there, in stillness, and for that stillness to be *all*. A rapture. A way of being you will never know. An extinct order of feeling altogether.

It walked the world, this extinct order, and then left it. The sea spray fades, the room returns. He is *there*. They are still, apart from the rise and fall of their breathing. And in that stillness every sound that the night throws up: the dove in the eaves, the stream in full flow, the squeak of the inn's sign in the wind – all have a purity, as if she's only just learnt to hear.

There they were; there they are. Just like any couple. Ordinary. And there is a kind of union in this night that legitimises the ring on her finger and carries with it the solemnity of a kind of marriage. One that will do, she tells herself, until nights like this will come with the close of every day. He rolls over. She watches. The mind of Europe is rolling over in bed. The mind of Europe is asleep. Become what it always was: the child rocking in its nursery to the rhythms of the Mississippi; to the tolling sea bell heard from the summer house on Eastern Point; to the low groan of waves breaking on granite rocks.

As much as she is determined to stay awake, she feels herself drifting off. And as she watches the sleeping Tom, her breathing falls into rhythm with his. The purr of the dove the last thing she hears.

* * *

When she wakes again it is to an animal whimper, and for a moment she is convinced there is an animal in the room. He is twitching: arms, body and legs. A fit? Some sort of condition he has kept from everyone? Suddenly, she is awake and alert. Then she realises he's dreaming. A bad dream. And the animal whimperings are the whimpers that come to us in nightmares.

Instinctively, she rises from her end of the bed, and, on her knees beside him, watches, unsure what to do. Her instinct is to give comfort. To soothe the twitching figure. But she is unsure. Does she have the right? And what if he should wake? He whimpers again, and impulse takes over. She leans over him and places comforting arms around him while resting her cheek on his chest. And for the first time in her forty-eight-year-old life, Emily Hale lies down with another human being. For that short time (less than a minute, for the nightmare does not last long), her body and his become one, and she knows what it is to be joined to someone else. And not be alone. There is more bliss in that moment than she has known all her life. For it occurs to her, a thought that only clarifies itself later, that the state of being alone is something that we might become numb to. And that one's loneliness can be large, like one's pain, until we cease to notice it at all. It is simply our way. Until a moment such as this. And though short-lived, it is the kind of moment from which she draws strength, the kind of moment that will make whatever follows more bearable.

She holds him in her arms. The whimpers fade. He does not wake. She has banished the nightmare. And at some point that blissful sense of union, of being joined to another, and that feeling of it being *all*, gradually gives way to desire. For it was impossible, after all those years, not to let lone desire, lone delight, finally have its way. As she stares down at his face, made younger, it seems, by sleep, eyes kiss. And then she lowers her face, and lips kiss. She leaves her lips on his only for as long as she dares without waking him. And as she lifts her lips from his she is light. Made weightless by the daring of her kiss. And seems to float back to her side of the bed. The nightmare banished. The Furies gone. Tom, once again, is sleeping the deep sleep of the child. And, she imagines, when he wakes he will remember only the dream of being kissed by a soothing Beatrice, when, all the time, it was *her*.

She could sing. There are ways of knowing someone: their talk, their manner, their little tell-tale signs that let you know something is wrong or something is right. But is there anything closer than this? The young, the young ... Surely, she tells herself in the darkness, she has known him now, as surely as any wife or lover. In a way that another age, one that *feels* differently, will find impossible to comprehend. He is *her* Tom again. And always will be now. For if every moment can contain a lifetime of living, then a lifetime can be contained in a moment. And this is hers.

* * *

The salty wind fans her face. Only moments survive. But what happens when the memory fails and the moments die? Who will be there to say: *this* is how it happened? That one summer's day a middle-aged couple took off in a borrowed car, drove into a storm, and took refuge in a country inn for the night. A night that inquiring scholars and biographers in years to come will all agree never happened. *Could* never have happened. One the world must never learn of or think possible. For he was a married man. She rubs the satchel hanging from her shoulder. The rocks near. Not long now, not long ...

In the early hours of the next morning, while Tom was slowly emerging from the deepest of deep sleeps, all nightmares banished, she went downstairs as the sun spilled over the rolling green hills in front of her, sat down, and, in her journal, the one she now carries in her satchel, recorded every single detail of the night before she forgot, carefully writing down the date of the entry at the top of the page: June 31st, 1939.

* * *

The drive back, by a different road, is silent. There are no games. The waters have receded, the bitumen is dry. The journey swift. A blue sky stretches from one side of the country to the other, the sun climbs towards midday. But Tom sees none of this. Tom is thinking. She knows he is and can almost hear it. But thinking what? The mind of Europe has much to ponder. But not, she imagines, the limitations of Byron, Milton and Tennyson. All essays he has recently written and which he sent her, as he always does. And as much as she reads them for what they say about their subject, she is always on the look-out for those private references that are always there, those flashes of the private man, the private life, intended for one reader only, like coded messages beamed out to her across the sea.

He has much to ponder, but not any of that. When he woke did he remember the dream of being kissed? The memory of a dream figure, a Lady of silences in a white gown, banishing the Furies from his sleep? Soothing the brow of troubled sleep and silently withdrawing? For just as he beams out private, coded messages across the sea to her in his writing, she is there in the poems too. She knows she is. And as much as she would never call herself a muse, as much as she would never claim such a title (for that would be beneath the white Lady of silences) she knows that's what she is. But she never makes claims and she never steps from the timeless into the cold light of day. For there she would dissolve. She is a dream.

And it is this, Emily is sure, that Tom is pondering. For the kiss was no dream, nor was the embrace. But he thinks it was. Can he have the Lady as she is (issuing instructions like the Boston sergeant major that Mrs Woolf takes her for, laughing too loudly or brazenly wearing a dress with all the colours of a country garden) and keep the dream? Indeed, he is not the only one pondering this. Their thinking is loud, each aware of the other, and each aware that at some point they must speak their thoughts. But not with the air rushing over their faces, and with the noise of the engine. They must eventually, she tells herself again, speak their thoughts, not shout them.

And so, in what she takes as mutually agreed silence, both possibly pondering the same question, the lead foot of the Lady in white steps on the gas, and in what seems little or no time they are entering the high street of the town. They pull up at the front of their cottages and Emily slowly turns round to Tom. Where to from here? He is pondering the road, then looks back at her.

'This is my promise,' he begins, 'that one day you will have your wish. One day *we* will. When the time is right.' He pauses and looks out the windscreen, watching the people of the town going this way and that, incidental as ants, then turns back to her. 'You remember when I came to see you just before I left for Oxford?'

She nods, of course she does.

'That day I came to ...' He stumbles, and she can see he stumbles because the memory of that day is still difficult, the pain still fresh. 'I came,' he resumes, once more watching the ants on the street, 'to profess my love. You know that. You knew that.'

Yes, yes. She knows. She knew. But the world annoyed her that day and she sent him away. And has there not been a day, has a day not passed since, when she has not wished herself back into that garden and given him the response he came for that their lives might begin again?

'Those feelings,' he continues, 'are ... are still there. Older, for much has happened, but still there. And this is my promise, that you shall have what you wish for. When the time comes.'

And they both know what he means: when the time comes. Were they ever allowed to forget that he was married; that she was a dream, and a secret one? And wasn't there always, stronger or fainter depending on the day, that constant feeling of contending with overwhelming odds: two modern players in an ancient drama that never gave them a chance? History, society, manners, the very times they inhabited, as well as the constant of an annoying world that never, and has never, just let people be.

But not this morning. This morning is bright with hope. This morning comes with a promise, and the hope that, against all odds, they just might win out, after all.

* * *

The sea spray whips her face, the rocks near, and Emily looks up at the cloudy sky above the open sea to where the great event of the beast crouches: tense, impatient, ready to spring. Or was it springing all the time, a pounce that was decades in the doing? Did they have their great event, and was it continually unfolding, there in front of them all the time?

* * *

Tom stops speaking and reaches out his hand for hers. 'This is my promise.'

She raises his hand and kisses it. The longed-for moment in the garden revisited, recreated in the front seat of a borrowed roadster. And her smile brightens. Wide and unrestrained. How … how American, after all. How wonderfully, wonderfully American of them, after all.

'Mr Eliot,' she says.

'Miss Hale?'

'We Boston ladies take promises seriously.'

'And in Missouri, Miss Hale, a man does not make a promise lightly.'

'I should hope not, Mr Eliot, because, when the time comes, I will hold you to that promise.'

They step from the roadster, collect the rug and picnic basket, and, walking side by side, her head resting on his shoulder, they enter the cottage, where her aunt and uncle rise from their chairs with questions of where they have been and seeking reassurance that all is well. She observes a momentary frown on Tom's face: a look that says, oh, *you*. I'd forgotten. But it passes as quickly as it appears. And Emily, placing the hamper on the lounge-room table, quickly assures them that, indeed, all is well.

It is then that they tell Tom that he has parcels and business waiting for him at the post office and that his office in London has called. He nods, turns to the three of them, then makes his way to the door he has only just entered, adding as he leaves that he shouldn't be long.

* * *

Upstairs, from her room in the next door cottage, she watches him, walking up the high street, looking down, his pace slow and unhurried, like a man savouring and prolonging a moment, unwilling to leave it or lose it.

He fades from view. At the same time she sees her aunt and uncle strolling up the street. Shopping. Or church. Or just walking. She is light. She is happy in a way she has never known before or thought possible. May even, she imagines, never be this happy again. And with that thought her lightness leaves her. A cloud passes over her, sudden and dramatic. Never this happy again ... And with it a single, insistent thought has now driven all others from her: he will weary of me. He will weary of the moment. Never this happy again ... neither him, nor her. Never again. Of this much she is certain. And in an instant. And of course, when he *does* weary of her, she will not hold him to that promise. How could she? No, she must act. She must simply banish the possibility of this ever happening and his ever becoming weary of her. Now. The previous night, this morning, the whole extended moment, she knows, is the culmination of a lifetime of waiting. She turns the ring on her finger round and round. She has known him now, surely, as well as any wife or lover. A beam has pierced her heart. And this, the ecstasy of Emily Hale, aged forty-eight, single, a stranger in a foreign land, is the culmination of a lifetime's longing and waiting. But he will weary of her. Surely. And this rapture, born of the knowledge that for one night she held him and cradled him and soothed him to sleep, banishing the Furies from his dreams, will dissolve with his weariness. And because it is all she has, she knows she must preserve it. Keep it from the ravages of weariness and time. So that whatever happens now, wherever their story takes them, she will always have this rapture, always have the ecstasy of the saints to sustain her, whatever follows.

She is leaving in a few days. Why not now? At the very height of their intensity. With the ache of his longing still sweet in his veins and hers. The Lady in white, silent and secret, must withdraw as she was always meant to.

Quickly she swings round to the wardrobe and the chest of drawers beside her bed, gathers a small suitcase and packs those things she needs. It doesn't take long. Packing never does. And within minutes she is standing in the lounge room of the cottage next door, hastily writing a note, saying she has been called away. Urgently. An invented phone call. A friend in London. No address. She writes Tom's name on the envelope, knowing he will tell her aunt and uncle. And with barely a glance around the room, she is on the street and walking towards the bus stop, just in time for the midday bus, for she has observed its departure on many occasions, only she never thought that one day she would be on it.

As the bus leaves she turns to look out the window, a glancing farewell to the town, and sees the distant figure of Tom making his way down the high street to the cottage, where her note will be waiting for him on the lounge-room table: Tom, her Tom again, head down, even paces; for all the world deep in the composition of a line or two. The bus passes the medieval market hall, familiar buildings and shops, and she sees them, Tom and Emily, Emily and Tom, everywhere she looks – pausing by a shop window, buying something at a market stall, greeting familiar strangers on the high street – Emily and Tom, the middle-aged couple that the town took them for. Wherever she looks, there they were; there they are. Looking back at her, observing her departure with pained surprise. And suddenly she rises and is on the point of calling out to the driver to stop. This is a moment of mad panic. What *is* she doing? But then she imagines the note on the table, Tom possibly reading it right now, her aunt and uncle entering the cottage to be told the news, and she knows she can't go back for she would look ridiculous: her ecstasy turned to farce. She has set these events in motion and is now controlled by them.

She slumps back into her seat, carried by the current, swept out of town by events that she herself initiated but which she is now powerless to stop.

* * *

Emily is standing barefoot on the deck. Her shoes are behind her, the rocks in front of her. Near and becoming nearer. The boat sways, the sea is rougher. And the storm clouds that have threatened to break all day roll round in the sky, rumbling. Henry keeps an eye on the waters in front of them, while also glancing back at the barefooted Miss Hale.

It is written. It was all written. Did she ever do anything that wasn't? Good Emily, proper Emily, who sang sweet songs in parlours, but who never really stepped beyond that parlour world onto a real stage because it was beneath her aunt, beneath her uncle, beneath *her*. For would not the clocks in all those parlours have stopped if she ever had? Would not time itself have ceased to tick out of sheer shame, the glass of the framed portraits of the country's elders have shattered on parlour mantelpieces across the city, and the street lamps have dimmed in disappointment? It was written. And when Tom draped her in a white dress, assigned to her a life of silent withdrawal and contemplation, there and not there, solid and a dream, Tom's Emily, never hers; when they made their pact of silence in an age of pacts, without as much as saying so to each other – was it not written too? *All* of it.

And where was Emily? *Who* was Emily? What did she become? In the end, nothing more or less than what was written. The Lady in white: withdrawn and withdrawing, faceless, her name lost in the writing. Was her life stolen, or did she hand it over? And while all this was taking place, while her life was being written, the Emily who was never recorded was just waiting to shed her white gown and step from myth into fact, bringing with her the gift of ordinary human love; just as she was waiting to shed her silence, because silence never came naturally to her. But she never did. And she never will. And what came to pass unfolded, it seems to her at the moment, with the inevitability of an ancient play. And as much as she told herself that if she was patient, and if she waited long enough, all would come to her, it never did.

She looks at Henry and she can see he's worried: about her, the sky and the waves slapping the side of the boat. And when he turns his wary gaze on her, what does he see? Trouble. Crazed eyes and trouble. A handful, crying out, 'Take me to them!' He's trapped. The sea is rough now, and he can't leave the wheel. And she's got the look of a woman who just might do anything. And as much as he might want to grab her and sit her down, he can't. He's invited a handful onto his boat. It's all over his face. His nervous, jerky movements at the wheel. He's heard the stories of the changed Miss Hale. In and out of hospital. Trying the patience of friends, and losing them. A changed Miss Hale from the one he last met years before; this is the barefooted, unwritten Emily, clutching her satchel.

As the rocks near and the boat continues to sway, she looks down at the satchel and opens it. And straight away all those faded letters with the faded stamps of dead kings appear to her. And her name on the envelopes: Emily Hale, at varying addresses across the country. She looks at the letters and looks to the sky and back again. I am Emily Hale, I am Emily … I am … There it is on the letters. That's who she is. In the poems she is the Lady; in the letters she is Emily. And they are all addressed to her in that familiar, slightly spiky writing. Words, writing, combed like his hair, neat and shiny. The memory of receiving all of them comes back, clear and strong. The thrill of simply looking at the envelopes even before opening them. Letters written during those years in which they lost each other. Some dozen or so. Letters, she has decided, that the world must never get its hands on. All making one mention or another of their night together, and all professing love at one point or another, or all the way through. And with passion. For she had left him with the longing still in his eyes, and that longing was poured into his letters. Letters the world must never see. As well as her journal in which their night together is faithfully recorded. For he was married, their night could never have happened, and she was a secret that only a handful of people knew about. That Boston woman. And as much as *she* knows what happened that night, the letters might tell a different story, as letters can. Could be read in all sorts of ways. Depending on who is reading them. And why they are reading them. And that would never do. For he was *her* Tom in the end. Always was and always will be her Tom. No matter the rash, the impulsive acts, no matter the years living in a foreign country trying to be something he never was, or the seas and years that separated them, *nobody* knew Tom the way she did. He was *hers*. He hers, she his: the young Tom who gazed in wonder at her across his cousin's parlour, the broken Tom who fell into her arms in the market square, the Tom who stepped out from the cottage in the town with the longing still in his eyes, and whom she left that way. The *only* woman he ever loved!

And it is that love, and the incumbent duty of love, that now brings her to these rocks, closer by the minute. Nobody, not in their hearts, in all of that stuffy island he chose to live in, with its stuffy towns and closed circles fixing you in judgement over combs of homemade honey, ever knew Tom the way she did. The way that Boston woman did. The only woman he ever loved! And it's all in these letters that the world must never see. For the world would talk, the wrong talk; the world would pry; the world would cheapen everything with its touch and destroy all she has left and all they ever had. And so the

Lady will maintain her silence. The Lady will be true. To the very end.

And it is at this point that she reaches for the letters, and clutching them, waving them in the air, runs barefoot to the railing, the wet smack of a wave slapping the side of the boat as she does, catching her, rocking and tripping her, leaving her falling forward onto the railing itself and peering down into the grey waters. All in a flash. And for a moment, in shock but oddly calm, hazy but clear, she longs for those waters. For the oblivion of those waters. Yes, yes, a watery death! And for those few moments she feels herself hovering between two worlds, finely balanced on the edge of the known and the unplumbed salty sea, noting at the same time, with an odd detachment, that she is still clutching the letters. Then she feels the arms of Henry around her waist, pulling her back towards the cabin, slowly inching his way across the deck, for he is old now and she is at this moment, she knows, and can't seem to help it, a dead weight.

'We're too old for all this, Miss Hale,' Henry calls out, the boat drifting. 'Much too old.'

And he has no sooner grabbed her from the railing and put her down on the deck than he has returned to the wheel, left spinning. How long did it take? How long was she hovering before he noticed? A few moments only, but the boat has been carried close to the rocks with the incoming tide, and as the waves break and recede from them, she can clearly see their bared teeth. You have come, and we have waited. All this time. Henry swings the wheel; the boat veers, describes a slow, arduous arc and gradually puts the rocks behind them as they begin the return journey. She meant only to fling the letters into the sea, into these waters that were Tom's and which meant so much to Tom. Return that which was Tom's to Tom. And in a place that, she was sure, he would be waiting to receive them. These rocks. But that's not how it will look and that's not how it will be told: in the town, and in the streets of Cambridge. A wave hit the boat, she tripped and fell. An accident. But that's not how it will be told. And the town will talk. It's a fishing town and trades in talk as much as it trades in fish. And the talk will spread to the streets of Cambridge, and on to her town. Concord will hear of this. She can tell from the pronouncement 'trouble' clearly stamped in Henry's eyes. He steers them homeward, against the tide. The boat labours, but the rocks eventually recede, the teeth withdraw.

Her face, hair and clothes are wet. She recalls hovering between one world and another for a few moments, fascinated by her own predicament, almost resigning herself to fate and whatever might happen; fate eventually arriving in the form of Henry. Now she is sitting on the deck, clutching the letters, her name smudged and blurred by the sea, the stamps of dead kings curled at the edges. And the hand that was set to hurl them into the sea and destroy them once and for all – an offering to the rocks, to Tom – although shaking (and she is registering the trembling over her whole body only now), gently places them back in the satchel. It is written.

The Lady leans her head back against the cabin. The sky rumbles, but never breaks. Lightning flares, but never strikes. The beast forever crouches, but never pounces. Or was it pouncing all the time, a leap decades in the doing? Henry looks round at her from time to time. What does he see? A handful, that's what. The Lady is a handful. No white gown, no May-time blossom, no pastoral scene. No Beatrice. Just the Lady herself, half drenched, slumped on the deck of an old fishing boat. She closes the satchel and draws it to her chest. What of it? What if posterity should one day get its grubby hands on them? What of it? Her name, though blurred and smudged by the sea, will be there for all to read. And Tom's. And the intimate details of their pact, like old, bound agreements between long-gone governments or countries, will be opened to the daylight of another age and speak to a changed world that will see things differently. And they will hear of a night that, as far as scholars and the world alike are concerned, never happened, *could* never have existed, but which nonetheless did; and which now exists in its own time: June 31st, 1939. A time that defies the clocks and calendars, like those evenings that feel as though they have already happened even as they are unfolding, and will again.

PART THREE

Lay Down Your Weary Tune

9.

It was just over there behind the trees on Eastern Point, for there were trees by then, after the war. The woods had grown back. And other houses had been built. Some hidden, some in clear view, even from here where Emily sits slumped on the deck of the boat, the satchel, with its contents, drawn close to her chest.

It was just over there in one of those hidden houses that she stayed in while she waited for Tom to complete the short walk from the family home to her. He had given her his promise, and she'd left him with the longing in his eyes. Nine years before. And although it felt then that her departure had been written, like everything else, now she's not so sure. Perhaps, perhaps that was the one moment that was *not* written: when she broke from the Lady's script, and *Emily* acted. Perhaps her leaving was the one thing that was not expected of her, the moment when the hidden authors of her life lost control for a few days and she stepped out of character: her stolen season when, however briefly, *she* controlled events. But nine years is a long time, and they were long years with, for the most part, only letters between them, a few of which (the ones she couldn't bear to part with) she holds to her chest; the others, most of them, long dispatched to Princeton. And they will stay there until another age that sees things differently will open them and read the story of Tom and Emily. How they came so close, but never came near.

Nine years. And at the end of those years she sat just over there in a rented house on Eastern Point and waited for Tom. They had met, of course, after the war. Had met often enough and sifted through what was left of *them*: what they had and didn't have.

This is my promise, he had said. When the time comes, he had said. I shall hold you to that promise, Mr Eliot, she'd added. Boston ladies don't take promises lightly, and Missouri men don't make them lightly. And now, the time had come. For the wife, and after all this time she still finds it difficult to say her name, the wife whom he'd not seen since she went into an asylum before the war, had died. He was, as the phrase goes, a free man.

She looks to the sky: had he ever been free? Wasn't he always running from one thing or another? Always being pursued by one thing or another, something he saw but which you didn't? Furies of the mind. And his wife, real as she was, became one of them. Until she died, and having died was no longer one of the Furies. No, then she was just a thin, frail and scared woman. For although Emily never met her, she has studied photographs of her and heard talk of her to the point that she feels she knows something of her. To the point that she has *her* Vivienne. There, she's said it. *Her* Vivienne, a girl really, doing her best to grow up so that she wasn't always a social embarrassment, but always feeling as though she was. And the more she felt that way or was made to feel that way, the more she lashed out, and the more things stayed the same. Then she was gone. And Emily would rather have had her alive, after all. For being dead, she was more powerful than ever. No one could touch her. She was no longer *that* woman. She was beyond such things. And being dead, she was more present than ever. Head in hands he sat, so she heard, the morning he was told she was gone, head in hands, saying, what have we done, what *have* we done? And through the tears, not a second, he said, not a second of happiness to look back on. Oh God, oh God, what *have* we done? What have *I* done! Head in hands, all through the morning he was told. Or so she heard. Head in his hands, and his mind absorbed with that one question only: no room for anyone or anything else. Yes, she would rather have had her alive, after all.

All the same he was now, as the phrase goes, a free man. But the phrase is meaningless. When was he ever free? When were they?

He visited after the war and they drove places in her Ford roadster. Meticulously maintained. *Their* car: to Gloucester, to Rockport, to the rocks of his youth. He came to Vermont in the summer to see her perform, and together they drove to Wood's Hole with friends, where she took the snap that now, framed, sits on her sideboard in the lounge room. But throughout it all, it was understood that their time had not yet come. There was a 'tomorrow', whatever form that tomorrow might take, waiting somewhere out there for them, and their days together, the small talk and banter, were sustained, at least for Emily, by the expectation of that tomorrow. He visited her, they stepped out. Heavens, she may even have displayed him to the world in a way she could never do in England, fuelled the rumours about Miss Hale and Mr Eliot among her girls, in schools in various parts of the country. She shakes her head now, slumped on the deck, her once luxuriant hair tangled and wet from sea spray.

But the time had come. A lifetime of waiting had come to this: a promise made almost nine years before. It was just over there, behind the trees, where she sat by a window and waited for Tom. A clear view of the dirt road he would come along.

And from her first glimpse of him she knew something was wrong. He was wearing the tweed suit with the short pants and the long socks and the tweed cap that she knew so well, almost like a golfer seeking some lost ball, lost after some rash shot years before. But as much as she should have been comforted by the familiarity of the suit ... Mr Eliot, you look *so* English ... the face was all wrong. This she could see, even from the window. And this first impression was confirmed with every step that drew him nearer to her, and finally brought him to her door.

She had met him twice since his wife's death, meetings in which they continued to circle the thing they most wanted to say, as, indeed, they had in that Cambridge garden years before. She barely knew what she thought any more, except that this morning, among all the uncertainty and awkwardness, would mark the end of the waiting. One way or another. But what to say? And how to say it? Would the beast pounce now? Would the beast bide its time a little longer? Or would it retreat into the jungle from which it came? Knowing that he was leaving soon (always leaving, she smiles, always leaving, and soon), they resolved to approach the thing itself and prod the beast. So he asked to meet her this morning, and there was something in the manner of his asking on the telephone that suggested something more than a stroll. And so, there they were. And there they are, just over there, in a house behind the trees.

His face is still all wrong as he steps in the door. She has removed her chair from the window, for she does not want to be seen by it, does not want to be the woman who sits and waits at windows. She rises as he enters and he grasps her hand and greets her, she can't help but feel in the circumstances, with absurd formality. He then lets go. Arms that would embrace hang by his sides, lips that would kiss mouth polite greetings about the house and the room and the view. As though they'd met only recently. He looks pale, weak, even sick. In no condition for a talk such as they must have. But have it they must. And so she begins, in a way that suggests that this is all part of one continuing conversation and that they are picking up the threads where they left off.

'Where were we, Tom?' She goes back to her chair and sits. 'Going round in circles, if I remember correctly.'

He sits in silence, staring at the wall, and she looks at him, willing him to say something. But the silence drags on and on. So much so that the gulls' cries outside, one tapering into another, enter the room and speak for them. And just when she thinks that this is it, this is the extent of his talk, that he is content to let the gulls talk for them, he turns to her.

'Emily,' and it is as though her name has become difficult for him to say, as, indeed, when they were first reunited, he had found it difficult to say his wife's name. The wife they still find it difficult to talk about and who has been mentioned only once by Emily and not again, as Tom had flinched at the sound of her name. But, it becomes apparent, it is not simply her name that is difficult; everything he says is difficult. 'I have loved you all these years. You know this.'

She stiffens, back upright, looking out over the room. 'I was led to believe as much.' And the moment she says this she regrets it. Why, why did she say 'led to …'? It's what her aunt would have said. He will think she believes he deceived her. Deceived himself. Led her on. When she knows full well that there is infinitely more to it than that. And always was.

'Yes, correct.'

'That's not quite what I meant.'

'I know, we never say quite what we mean.'

'Only afterwards.'

'Sometimes.'

He looks at her, as if to say that for too long they have never quite said what they meant, and that for once they must, and he will. For his whole manner suggests that he cannot leave until it is said.

'And I shall continue to love you. One doesn't simply stop loving.'

Here he pauses, and she lets him be, for a feeling as hopelessly solitary as the tapering sound of the gulls tells her that a long-dreaded moment of finality is upon her, and nothing she can do will change it. Who led whom on? Who followed whom? What dance did they invent?

Tom continues. 'No, one doesn't simply stop loving. But ...' and here Emily's eyes close, mimicking the way she would dearly love to block her ears, '... but the moment of that love has passed. *It's too late.*' If he looks to her for a reaction, he sees only her closed eyes. 'I know,' he resumes, 'I once promised you that when the time came you would have what you wished for. It was a solemn promise, given in absolute sincerity. And I have no regret for saying it, for I meant what I said at the time. But I have come this morning to ask to be released from that promise.'

Here he stops, and almost slumps in his chair from the effort of having spoken. Her eyes are shut. She says nothing, then finally opens them to a changed world and imagines asking: And if I were to say 'no', and hold you to that promise?

He is looking down at the floor, and she is free to observe him. English tweeds, cap in hand. Old, but somehow young.

For he was always an old young man, and now he's a young old man. And behind the grave and pale face, she can still see the Tom she first met in his cousin's parlour. The impish, the Gioconda smile may be gone, but its shadow is still there. At least, for Emily. For she too feels herself to be an old young woman and a young old woman. And their times, *all* their times, now seem to converge in front of her. And in that instant they are the sum total of what they were and what they are and what they might have been, all at once: their life together compressed into a moment, like a jumbled portrait. The image lingers, then fades into a long, lingering silence. She will hold him captive with her silence, punish him with silence, for as long as she chooses. The Lady, it is understood, will decide when they are done. And so, powerless, he waits.

'Oh, Mr E, Mr E ...' she says, shaking her head slowly, a ghostly chorus of parlour laughter accompanying her words as Tom looks up to the ceiling in silent remembrance. 'I had feelings for you, I had *such* feelings for you. And still do. And it seems I was foolish enough to hope that when the time was right these feelings could be set free. Silly Emily, she mustn't hope for things that may never happen.' She pauses, staring at Tom, who is still gazing at the ceiling as though some clue, some figure in the patterning that would clarify everything, were to be found there. He wishes he wasn't here, she's thinking. He will sit, he will listen, but his manner (an attitude of resignation that if he *must* listen, listen he will) is that of someone whose mind is elsewhere. As though he has already moved on, and this whole conversation were just an unavoidable formality. He is changed. Gone cold on her. Detached himself. This she sees in an instant, as if a blindfold had been ripped from her. And at the same time, she is asking herself, how long, how long has this been the case? And when Emily resumes the wistfulness is gone and there is a new hardness in her voice. 'Silly Emily, she waited all these years for this?' Still he remains impassive, even resolute. And her voice rises as she continues. 'Do you not think she deserves more?' She thinks to herself, I was your silent Lady all those years. I waited an eternity to step from the shadows into the light and speak my name. But now, it seems, I never will. Her voice rises again. 'Do you not think *I* deserve just a little more than this?' Still he remains silent, unmoved. A frown creases his forehead. He squirms in his seat: he is discomforted, yes — but not moved. Discomforted by her fate — but that is all. Then something breaks, something snaps. A lifetime of mannered decorum comes crashing down. And suddenly, the Lady of silences erupts into undignified command. 'Look at me!'

He jumps in his chair and turns to look upon her. And while she notes there is alarm in his look, she also detects concern, even pity. Something, at least, she thinks. At least there's that.

He shakes his head. 'Emily, Emily … no one knows more than I do that you deserved and deserve infinitely more. And I dearly wish I still had it to give. But,' and here his gaze returns to the pattern in the ceiling then to her, 'I no longer do. It's too late.'

She rocks in her chair, back and forth, a groan rising from her, low and continuous, like the groan of the rocks themselves, long and continuous, sigh upon sigh, finally exploding into tears. And when she resumes, her voice is like no voice he, or she, has ever heard issue from her; choking on tears, the words are not so much uttered as expelled from her. And tears? Tears, for heaven's sake. The room, she imagines, is almost embarrassed. What does she think she is doing? This is a 'scene', and such scenes, it has always been understood, are beneath these rooms and the people they were built for. All the same, a scene it is and a scene it shall be. And so, choking on tears and catching her breath between utterances, she fills the air with words that have waited too long to be heard. 'Silly, silly Emily, who gave you the best years of her life!' She pauses a moment for breath, chest heaving. 'There was a man in Concord,' and here she looks directly at him with steely, accusing eyes, 'who kept his mistress for twenty years throughout a long, loveless marriage. And when his wife died, the wife for whom he felt absolutely nothing, do you know what he did? He *married* her! And isn't that just so wonderful and noble and sweet, to do that for the woman who gave him the best years of her life! And all through those years when I put my life on the shelf and left it there for you, when I handed my life over, I thought of that man and the sweetness of what he did, and I told myself over and again that my Tom, my Tom too will be noble and sweet and true. Oh, what fools,' she continues in this voice that is guttural, almost elemental, and like no voice that has ever issued from her, 'what fools we are! Silly, silly Emily, who waited a lifetime for this. Do you not think, do you not imagine in some small part of you that you too are bound to your promise to be sweet and noble and true? Is this it?' And that final *it* cracks like the thunder above Henry's boat, at once reverberating across the sky over the open waters off Eastern Point and around the room.

And as the word claps in his ears, Tom swings round as if awoken. And his voice, harsh and, it seems now, pitiless, the voice of one who sees her tears but not her pain, is, likewise, unlike any voice she ever heard come out of him. 'I would have given you *everything*! Everything! I would have married you in an instant. Given myself unreservedly. Walked throughout the years with you, wherever they took us. I too had that kind of certainty. And I too waited. A young fool with more feeling than sense!' His voice rises and soon he is shouting, a lifetime's messy emotions rising from the depths they have long been consigned to, the distant pain as strong as yesterday. 'Once! I loved you once. You know so well I did. Love like faith. Pure and simple. And I came to you with that love. To give it to you. To place it in your care. And all I required was a word. A confirmation that I was not dreaming. That I was not ridiculous. That I was not a fool. But you turned away. Or you turned me away. You saw it all and still you turned away!' He stands, glowering at her. Oh, what have they become? Is he really yelling, is she really shouting? How has this come about? This can't be them. Not Tom and Emily. Can they just begin again? Start this all over? But no, they can't. Of course not. Like some long, rumbling dispute that erupts into inevitable war, it must now be seen through. 'Here, I said,' and he thumps his chest as he speaks, '*this* is for you. And I will happily go with you all my days. Where was your heart?'

Yes, he is yelling. And as Tom's voice rises, as Tom himself has risen, so too does Emily. Both facing each other. And these two characters from the pages of Mr James or Mrs Wharton – their lines written before they ever spoke, their roles assigned, their characters moulded by the invisible author of the time and the place that made them – are now shouting and yelling and glaring across the room as if they no longer recognised each other, no longer knew who they were. Or rather, they are beginning to recognise that had they been assigned an author from another age, they might well have set free all these feelings that they had never dared let break the surface, set them free a lot sooner, and *this* is what they would have become. And these are the words they might have spoken.

'I was not myself that day!' she cries and pleads, both begging and demanding to be understood: see my tears, and see my pain. 'You come to me once and once only and offer up your heart and I'm supposed to jump and say, yes Tom, yes Tom. All our days, Tom! Just like that,' she cries, clapping her hands together. 'But it was the wrong day. The right love, but the wrong day. And don't you think there hasn't been a day gone by since when I haven't looked deep into myself, into the workings of my heart, and wished that day back to live all over again? Don't you? Don't you think I haven't relived that day over and again ever since? Well?' She stops, exhausted, swaying on her feet and steadying herself on the arm of the chair. She stays like this until she feels strong enough to go on, and when she resumes her voice is softer, the anger wrung from her. 'But I was not myself that day. Don't you think I know it?' The question is addressed to herself as much as Tom. 'And is it fair that just a handful of hours should amount to so much?'

He shakes his head, as if to say what they both know, that the fairness or unfairness of such things is not the point. His voice too is softer, drained of any lingering indignation. 'Had I known, had I left that day knowing that you had such feelings for me as I had for you, I would never have stayed away. Would never have married. Would always have come back, with yellow roses for Miss Hale. If I had known there were something to come back to, I would have. And there was. But I never knew then.'

'And I,' she says, almost smiling, 'I would have waited, knowing that a year isn't so long, after all.' And here she does smile, with a grim resignation. 'And now our time has come and gone, and I have waited all these years. For *this*.' She slumps back into her chair.

Tom eases back into his. 'I know it was I who left, but I was the one who *felt* left. And I know we didn't have long together, but I imagine that sometimes an hour is enough. Or a minute. All I know is that afterwards I had this constant, nagging feeling that I was lacking an arm or leg, or some vital part of me, and would have to go through life with the feeling that something that was once there was now gone, and all I would be left with would be the sensation of when it was there.' He stares at her, she at him, long and deep: her eyes bright with music, his the darkest eyes she has ever looked into; both lingering, just as they had in the parlour games of their youth, one last time, as the ghost of old love passes between them and slowly, reluctantly, leaves the room.

'*That* was our time,' she murmurs. 'Never to be repeated.'

'No.'

'Too late.'

With no further delay, drained and exhausted, she raises her arm almost regally. 'You are released.'

His eyes close as he absorbs the finality of what has happened. Of what she has said. What have we done ... what have we ... ? He sits perfectly still, saying nothing, for some time. Then without uttering another word (for what else is there to say?), he rises from his chair and lets himself out. No goodbye, no final farewell: from either him or her. They are beyond such things.

They pass the lighthouse, the wharf Henry and Emily started from now visible in the distance. Emily is still on the deck, more or less where Henry placed her. She is contemplating the land as Eastern Point passes by. There, just over there ... They were the last words they ever exchanged. *You are released.* The last time they ever sat in the same room together and talked. The last time *he* ever spoke to *her*. The last time they ever met.

For all the shouting and accusation, a brief meeting after such a long wait. Letters had sustained them during the war and between his or her visits to here or there afterwards. But after that morning, there were only letters. And not many. There, just over there …

She hears the door click shut. He is gone. The room is silent. She takes her chair back to the window and studies the dirt road along which he came not so long before and waits for him to reappear. And soon he does. With his cap still in hand, he retraces his steps towards the family's old holiday house. And it occurs to her that this is the last time she'll ever see him. The last time their paths will ever cross. For she is not one of the family (never *felt* one of the family), and never will be now. And she will have no cause to ever return to this place. They will live, in all likelihood, in separate worlds.

Perhaps he will turn, and look back just once. Does he know he is being watched? Possibly. He doesn't turn. And the fact that he doesn't, she takes as a pronouncement. This is final. *Final*, that dreaded word. His steps are even, steady. Familiar tweeds, familiar Tom, familiar for the last time. Her Tom for the last time.

Then a young couple, the woman in summer frock, the man in summer suit, appears and the three of them pause and talk. The young couple seems to be asking where something or other is, and Tom points them in the right direction. The two young people are smiling as they chat; the talk continues, becomes an exchange – perhaps they have discovered places and people in common. And so, on they chat, the young people smiling. There is even time for a cigarette. And Tom, drawing, no doubt, on one of his French cigarettes (and she can almost smell it from where she sits), waves his smoking hand here and there in the morning sun: and was that a smile? A happy man, she thinks. A man who looks, for all the world, like someone who has just had a giant weight taken off him and is enjoying the lightness he now feels. Soon they part and wave each other farewell. Like old friends. Then he turns, head bowed once again, solemn once again, and concentrating on each step as he would on the words for a poem, he passes round a small bend in the road and disappears. The great event.

And it is then that the upright posture, the straight upright back of Emily Hale, gives way and her head slumps forward, no longer looking out the window, for there is nothing to look at. Or for. Who was he? Who *is* he? This man who stands and chats and smokes in the morning light without a care: the lightness he feels, the lightness that comes of being released from the weight of his promise, animating his every gesture and movement. A happy man, she thinks, unaware that his happiness has been noted. Who was he? Did she *ever* know? All the years, all the waiting; the deals that were never acknowledged as deals; the things you told yourself that you only half believed at the time and which, now, you can't believe you told yourself at all; all the hopes that were only ever false – all have come to this. Where else? It was always coming to this, already had and would again.

She claws at the ring on her finger. But it's wedded to her skin and won't budge. Wedded to her very being. She pulls on it again and again, finally dragging it over her knuckle and wrenching it free. In tears of utter misery, she throws it across the room so that it ricochets from floor to wall and back to the floor, ringing hollow, hollow and empty, like all the promises and unspoken deals. Like all the hollow years that never amounted to anything. It settles, rattling to a stop. She rubs her finger, her whole body aches for what has been wrenched from her, what sustained her all these years ... She's been used. Used all along. And all the talk of pure love was as hollow as the sound of the ring bouncing from wall to floor, like a ten-cent toy, a ten-cent love, a cheap imitation of the real thing.

Pure love, she spits the phrase into the air. Pure? She could almost laugh. Not so pure that it couldn't be dragged down from the heavens and put to work, not so pure it couldn't be soiled by ambition and ordinary, everyday lust: lust that paraded itself as art. And every morning when he knelt and worshipped this God of his, murmuring words of love, purity and light, was he not also worshipping at the altar of cheap, everyday fame, and was she not the very sacrifice, the very thing he used to get it? And, having got it, he now has no further need for her.

The ring lies somewhere in the room. Let it rest wherever it fell. Tomorrow, the day after, next week, somebody will find it and pick it up and perhaps wonder how it got there.

The gulls call, their cries tapering into silence, then they call again, on and on, and once more that feeling of utter solitariness engulfs her.

With the lighthouse behind her and Eastern Point all but passed, Emily finds the strength to rise from the deck. The wharf from which they started their journey, hours ago, years ago, for it has been measured in both hours and years, nears. And as it nears, she notes that the feeling of utter solitariness that engulfed her that day never really went. That it is still with her, only she has grown used to it, and she's not sure whether to be thankful for that or not.

* * *

Miss Hale has her shoes on. Miss Hale stands steady on the deck. The water is smoother here. Henry is guiding them into the wharf, no longer, it seems, feeling the need to look over his shoulder every minute or so to check on her. But when he does she smiles. Thank you for your concern, Henry, the smile says; Miss Hale is doing fine now.

The town is close and becoming closer with every minute. She can even see her car now, parked in the street running along the harbour.

Too late. Yes, indeed. It was always too late: in a Boston garden; in a medieval marketplace with the sun low across the town; sitting on the boulders at the front of the family house, concealed now behind the trees on Eastern Point. Was there ever a moment when it wasn't too late?

One of those vaguely annoying phrases that are everywhere now comes to mind: *The moment was structured that way.* One of her students had used it in her last year of teaching: one of those vaguely annoying phrases by one of the new writers she's never read and never will. Why would she? She's walked with the best. All the same, like those annoying little jingles that are everywhere now, the phrase comes back to her. And it will do. May even be true. Was there ever a moment when they had a chance, or was everything a series of structured moments, and not by some invisible hand or author, but by that combination of who they were, when they were and where they were? Do we ever rise above that or leave that behind, or is every single decision and every single action written into us – and all we do is enact them?

As annoying as such phrases may be, she cannot deny that it was a similar thought that carried her through those years *after* Tom, and that she held on to when she fell apart. The belief that she had done everything she could, and that, in the end, it didn't really matter anyway: the result would have been the same. Indeed, she had written to a friend, during those long years after Tom, saying that even if their relationship had been consummated as these things are in the ordinary world of ordinary human love (a blunt way of putting it that she thought about before committing it to paper), would it have worked anyway? For the more she thought about it, the more she found it difficult, if not impossible, to conceive of them together. Only in make-believe was it possible. Another life altogether that they never lived, but could have. It was a way of telling herself that no matter what he or she had done, there was only ever going to be one ending. And it was already written from the moment they met.

As well as this, there was also that consoling feeling that they had both acted with a kind of tragic nobility. That they had been in conflict with forces greater than themselves – social, historical, geographical – and had, at least, fought nobly for a life that the world was never going to grant them.

But all that changed one January day in 1957. How did she learn of it? She's not sure now. Sometimes these things, learning of this or that event, are clear. Sometimes blurred, even confused, like imagining you were somewhere of historic moment when, in fact, you weren't. That day and the weeks following are a blur. She may have fainted. Did someone tell her; did she read it in the newspaper? Probably. In a newspaper, just like everybody else. 'Poet Marries his Secretary'. She may even have been amused for a moment. Thought of it as a distracting piece of gossip on a day of no news. Which poet? What woman? Then everything became a blur.

T.S. Eliot, aged sixty-eight, had married his secretary, Valerie Fletcher, aged thirty, at a registry office in London the previous morning. In a registry office, again. Secretly, again. Impossible! Not the same mistake twice. Not Tom, surely. Not *her* Tom. *Her* Tom would never behave beneath himself twice! But who was her Tom, after all? Did he *ever* exist? After more than forty years of parties, concerts, meetings, letters; after endless hours of sifting through what they had and didn't have; had she ever really known him at all? For until that day she could always tell herself that they had fought nobly for a life that the gods were never going to grant them. And that nobody knew Tom the way she did. The only woman he ever loved. In that way they were always noble; he was always noble and *hers*. For she had a deep, privileged knowledge of him that belonged to her and nobody else. Other people met him, but never knew him. Other people read him, but when *she* read him it was as though the writer and the reader were one.

And when she spoke of him, to her girls or to friends, it was always in the manner of one who possessed an intimate knowledge of the man that no one else did. And always with quiet confidence. So much so that everybody nodded solemnly whenever she made observations or pronouncements about him, such as, 'No, my dear, he would never say that. Not Tom. Or *do* that.' Pronouncements delivered with such authority that no one ever questioned her. Now, were they laughing? If she were to walk into a crowded room, would her friends, her associates, her girls, turn their heads briefly to wipe the smiles from their faces, before turning back to express their sympathy? Their *sympathy*!

And, once again, that feeling of being used, of having been used all along, came back to her. And she'd wished she still had the ring on her finger, just for the satisfaction of once more wrenching it from her, flinging it to the floor, and hearing it ring hollow in all its ten-cent glory.

Days, months, passed in a blur. And it has stayed a blur: the hospital that she ended up in; the bright corridors; the long, dark, sleepless nights. The memories of things that may or may not have happened, the way she imagined, or meant what she thought: a knowing look at a Sunday service; a smile; a passing, unguarded remark that may have been about her, or may not – such was the line between the real and the imagined. *Everything* was about her. And personal. Whether it was or it wasn't. And everything she'd known and come to take for granted was shattered: the Miss Hale, the Emily that she thought she was, defined by her years with her 'special friend'; the Tom she thought she knew as no other could, but whom others may well have known better. Everything was shattered. For in the end, who was she, and who had she been throughout all their years together: an actor playing out a role so completely and for so long that she forgot she was acting? And who was the Tom she had known? Was it all a shadow play? Illusions within lies within deceptions that we choose to believe? And which we do while the illusions are believable, until the lies, deception and the self-deception are unmasked and everything shatters and we fall apart. Become fragments. Broken springs, wooden limbs and glass eyes lying scattered and waiting to be reassembled. But by whom? And what new form should the retrieved remains take? Who was she, who was he, who were they? Did she ever know?

Henry is securing the boat to the wharf. When did that happen? When did they arrive? And just as he had tried to help her onto the boat, he now helps her off. Even secures the satchel strung over her shoulder, and she lets him. What of it? But he retains that look of concern, and speaks like an adult speaking to a child, the very old or someone who's had a bit of a shock.

'Can you drive?'

'Yes.'

It is not so long since he dragged her precariously balanced body from the boat's railing and placed her, shoeless, on the deck near the cabin, watching over her every available moment on the journey back.

'Let me.'

She shakes her head. 'I'm perfectly capable. Besides,' she says, looking up the wharf to her car, as distinctive on the street as the Boston ladies of her youth would be now, 'I have my chauffeur.'

With this, Henry frowns, puzzled, then follows her gaze and smiles. It is a reassured smile. It is the kind of comment that tells him that, yes, her mind is back.

She thanks him for everything. She hopes she hasn't been a bother, and he assures her that no, Miss Hale is never a bother. Besides, what else did he have to do today? And when she shakes his hand as she says goodbye (which it probably is), he watches her walk slowly, but deliberately, along the wharf to her car and climb inside.

The gulls call. In the front seat of the roadster she is perfectly still. For one, two minutes. Then the lead foot of Emily Hale revs the ancient beast into life and she hits the road as if pouncing onto it.

* * *

In the blink of an eye, he was gone. Except it wasn't the blink of an eye, it was seven years. Seven years which they experienced in opposite ways: hers the hollow years, banished from his life and putting the pieces of herself back together; his the happiest years, a second childhood.

The landscape passes in reverse order. The day folds back in on itself. The light mellows. T.S. Eliot, the poet, is dead in London at seventy-six, the newspaper report said.

'T.S. Eliot, the poet,' she mouths silently, watching the countryside pass. 'As apart from T.S. Eliot the trapeze artist, famous for the double back-flip that tragically ended his life.' She smiles. 'On a circus floor in St Louis, watched by hundreds in disbelief.'

'The same T.S. Eliot, Miss Hale.'

Every day he's *there*. At different phases of his life. Of their life. For it occurred to her in the months following the news that he has two widows: the one the world knows as Mrs Eliot, a title that, at times, seemed so near, but which was never hers; and the one the world knows nothing of. So completely had the Lady withdrawn in those last years. Or been withdrawn.

Written out of his life as if she never existed. All her letters to him destroyed, the last of which he never replied to. And where, in photos and snaps, she might once have stood beside him at a play opening in Vermont or Boston, he now quite possibly stands alone. It's the kind of bleak speculation she was prey to and still is sometimes. Doesn't take much to cut someone out of your life, she muses, just an iron will and a good pair of scissors. Not so much air-brushed as snipped from the photograph. Never existed, as far as the world is concerned. A footnote in some study, at best. All the same, she knows that T.S. Eliot, the poet, as apart from ... has two widows.

She met the woman once. Even liked her. Had resigned herself to the belief that this woman, whom she never knew existed until she read her name in the paper and thought for a moment, *who?*, had given him the happiness of a second childhood in a way that she never could have. *Too late.* Too late for Tom and Emily. Together they had waited and watched for the great event to reveal itself, when, all along, it *had* been slowly revealing itself. A leap so slow, so gradual, you barely noticed it. Like the changing colours of the day out there. Like the changing colours of the trees. Green, slowly and subtly turning vermilion. They had their great event, after all. It just wasn't what they'd thought it would be. And when you're not looking for something, it's easy to miss it.

And so, two widows met. But only one of them thought of it in those terms. And as much as she liked her, as much as she felt compelled by then to concede that this young woman – and oh, she was young – had done what she, Emily, could never have done, she was also left with the impression that the young widow had departed with an unspoken air of disappointment: as if to say, without ever saying so, that she'd expected more. Hadn't they all: that bony Woolf woman, the young poet who said clever things, even the marmoset that sat on Mr Woolf's shoulder? So too, this young woman expected more. So *this* is the Lady? This is her? It was as if the meeting, not long after Tom died, were a test – and she had failed.

But it was something the young widow said at the end of their chat that, above all, stayed with Emily. A calculated after-thought.

'I'm sometimes asked,' she said, picking up a biscuit, 'what it was like. Marrying an older man. What was it like, they ask,' she said with a smile as good as a wink. 'Well, I always say, he might have been half his age.' Here she popped the biscuit into her mouth.

It was said in a manner that clearly implied, this is just between you and me. A calculated after-thought masquerading as a confidence: a way of saying, whoever the Tom was that you knew, you never knew that. *That* Tom was mine. Then she was gone, and Emily saw the confident young wife in the confident young widow – as she closed her door, returned to the lounge room, and slumped into her chair, half-eaten cake and biscuit on the table, tea virtually untouched, contemplating precisely the same question the young wife and widow was often asked: what was it like?

All the same, she took to her and couldn't help but notice that they spoke of him in the same way: as though he weren't gone at all. As though he had just popped out. Would either be back any minute, or was just *there*. 'And I'd watch that lead foot of yours, Miss Hale. We're neither of us getting any younger.'

A smile flickers across her face. 'You're sure you're from Missouri, Mr Eliot? I felt positive ...'

But she never finishes the sentence. Sometimes it's as though he's just *too* present. And it's at those moments that she knows, more keenly than if he were a distant memory, that he's not. And at some point in the last few months, she decided not only had they had their great event after all, but that he was now and forever in her care. Whatever rights Mrs Eliot had over Tom, she had hers too. And it was a responsibility she took seriously. She is the Lady, after all. For in death, his nobility was restored. She was no longer used, she was immortalised. Their struggle, like an ancient play, was once more tragic. That was why the letters and the journal had to be destroyed, for the world would get its hands on them one day and cheapen everything, and that would never do. Or so she'd thought.

For when the moment came she couldn't fling them into that blue-grey sea. When she slipped and almost fell (and how did that look to Henry?), when the satchel almost went overboard, and for a moment looked like it would, her instinct took over instantly and she clasped it to her as if retrieving some vital organ, some part of her without which she couldn't continue to exist. And so the satchel and its contents come with her and go with her. And yes, yes, one day the world will get its hands on them, when everybody involved is long gone and can't be touched any more. And they will reveal to another age that those days, months and years that constituted their great event really did exist: that the Lady had a name. And is that so bad: so beneath him, beneath her, beneath *them*? Had she cared more, would they now be floating round the rocks before being swept onto the beach or out to sea, depending on the tide?

The shadows are long now as she enters the town, passing up the main street, past the doughnut shop, the antique store and the café (observing, as she goes, the figures of Grace and a young man she assumes to be the animal, watching her pass), then turning at the church and parking in the street opposite her cottage.

She steps from the car. The white paint of her cottage is mellow in the early-evening light. And as much as she's always felt right here, she also registered, from the first time she saw it, that it had a certain look of bland finality to it: the sort of place where you live out your days and where things end. Where things fizzle out. And she registers that thought again. Is this, in the end, what all the waiting was for: a cottage in Concord?

She closes the car door, the satchel over her shoulder. It's Wednesday. The Women's Parish Association meets tonight. And as she glances at the church across the green that divides her cottage from it, she sees that the lights are on and preparations are afoot. And for the first time since she joined the association (for she has never missed a night), she is asking herself if she can really be bothered after such a day, if the association could get by, just this once, without her. It is tempting, and she is almost tempted. But not really. She is Miss Hale. They will be expecting her. She must go.

Emily has just enough time to shed her summer dress, salty from the sea, and change. Inside, mindful of the time, she takes the contents of the satchel, the letters and her journal from years before, and hastily dumps them in the drawer of her desk where the payments for her classes are also kept. Spare, ready cash that she draws on without need of bothering with the bank. And as she opens her front door and looks upon the church opposite, she sees the familiar faces of the association arriving. Life! And once again, as she walks across the lawn to join them, she's asking herself, is this what the waiting was all for?

10.

Twilight is fading into evening as Emily Hale crosses the green verge to the church. She has changed from her sea-soaked dress into a white summer frock and her hair is combed back into a bun. Her feet, tucked into summer sandals, tread the lawn slowly. It is a thoughtful walk. Miss Hale has much on her mind.

She is mindful of the familiar Wednesday evening gathering making its way into the church and of evening falling, but is also troubled by the lingering image of herself precariously balanced on the boat's railing, of what might have happened, and what Henry might be thinking. And, more importantly, whom, if anyone, he might tell. Will Concord hear of the day's events? For she feels as though the name of Emily Hale is in the balance as well. A small community talks, and its talk may well travel in ever-widening circles to the outside world, where the behaviour may raise eyebrows. A disappointment for Tom, for he is walking beside her at this moment. She has never disappointed Tom. She was always above that. She had to be. She was Beatrice, she was the Lady; she had to remain so and must still remain so. A disappointed Tom is as inconceivable as a disappointed Dante. The Lady, in a white frock, is above such things. For if the subject of art becomes a spectacle, raises eyebrows and is found wanting, is not the art itself? Lines lavished on a disappointment become lesser lines. She bears high office.

So Emily Hale has much on her mind as she nears the church door and the Women's Parish Association meeting, and does not notice the car parked in the street opposite, where Grace and Ted observe her slow, thoughtful progress.

* * *

They have been there for ten or so minutes. Long enough to smoke another joint and for the dope to start taking effect. The air inside the car is thick. Grace is at the wheel. And as she watches Miss Hale, she is not sure if it is Miss Hale who is making seemingly drugged progress, or her own drugged senses at work. Then Miss Hale slips into the lighted doorway of the church hall and the door closes.

Grace and Ted look at each other. They are suddenly alert. Ted, with the clear dark eyes of a fox, nods. Now. He opens the car door, and in the hazy evening light, steals over the lawn, unseen. He slips from view. To the other side of the cottage, away from the street.

Time plods. The minutes are excruciatingly long. At some point, Grace becomes aware of the beating of her heart. Loud and insistent. Until she can't hear anything else. It feels as if it's about to explode from her chest. Ted will be looking for a cottage window that is unlocked, even open. But if there isn't one, or if he is just too stupid to find it, he will have to force a window. God! Takes time, she guesses. Too much of it. Could be noisy. She is at the wheel, ready to take off the moment he returns. But he is taking ages. She imagines him clambering in through the lounge-room window (which, all through summer, has been open), following her instructions, and crossing into Miss Hale's study, to her desk, where the money is kept, then retracing his steps. It should take no more than a couple of minutes. But he is taking longer, much longer. Something's wrong. It's a fuck-up. Of course, Ted's a fuck-up. How could it be otherwise?

She wills him, as if by telepathy. The desk. Right-hand side, you fool. Top drawer. Take the money and leave. Whether it's the effect of the dope stretching the minutes, or a slow, drugged Ted taking more time than he should, she can't be sure. But she is becoming increasingly convinced that something's gone horribly wrong. A car passes slowly. Her first thought is the police, and she eyes it warily. But it's just a car full of young locals out for a cruise. Her heart is still on the point of leaping from her chest, and in a moment of clarity she sees herself as she is at this very moment, sitting at the wheel of Ted's car, the engine running, and saying silently to herself: what on earth are you doing? What were you thinking? And she has no answer, for the truth is she wasn't thinking when she mentioned all of this to Ted, assuming he would forget. That the dope would do its work and he'd forget. But he didn't. And when he spoke to her about it, it was in a manner that suggested it was all decided. And somehow she couldn't muster the strength or the will to say no. So she just went along with it. And so here she is, at the wheel of the getaway car. It's a job. They're doing a job, for God's sake! What was she thinking? She wasn't thinking. And it's not as though they're robbing just anybody, they're robbing Miss Hale.

And while she waits, wondering what the fuck Ted is up to, she tells herself again and again that life isn't going to give Ted much. It's small change. Miss Hale won't miss it. Surely not, she tells herself, but doesn't believe a word. Whether Miss Hale misses or doesn't miss the money isn't the point. But what is? A car passes. No Ted. Another. And just when she's convinced something really has gone dreadfully wrong, she sees the stooped, shadowy figure of Ted stealing his way back across the lawn like the thief in the night that he is.

He bounds into the car and as soon as he closes the door she accelerates away. There is a loud revving of the engine, the squeal of tyres on the road, and Ted turns to her, yelling, 'Slow down.'

'What?'

'We're just cruising the town. Slow down!'

He's right. She slows. No cars about. No strollers. Lucky.

'What the hell took you so long?'

'I thought you said she keeps a window open.'

'She does.'

'She doesn't.'

'You didn't look properly.'

'I looked everywhere. I had to force one.'

'You what?'

'It was easy.'

'You found the desk, and the drawer?'

'Yeah.'

He pats his stomach, and for the first time she notices a small mound under his shirt. 'It's all there.'

'That's all money?'

He bursts out laughing. 'If only.'

'Then what?'

He's laughing and she's wondering what on earth he finds so funny.

'I just took the whole drawer.'

'The whole drawer?'

'Everything.'

'Just what did you take?'

'I dunno. I didn't have time to look.'

She shakes her head as they follow one street after another and slowly ease out of the town. Despite the dope, perhaps because of the dope, her hands are trembling. Her father will be driving back from Cambridge. God, her father. She can't begin to think about that. She ought to be home when he arrives. But it's no matter if she's not, she tells herself. She's a big girl now. All the same, she can't be too late. But she's tense, ready to snap. Ted sees this.

'Hey,' he says, 'relax. We did it! Whoo!'

With that he breaks into laughter again, and as much as her heart is pounding, and as much as she's asking herself what on earth she is doing, and who is this guy, anyway, she bursts into laughter at the sheer madness of everything. They just did a job, for God's sake. A job! And soon they're both laughing uncontrollably and she's forced to slow down even more. She winds down the window to let the evening air in. Ted winds his window down too. The rush of cool air blows the dope fog inside the car away, and it's almost as though she's been instantly sobered. They enter the countryside, the laughter subsides, and once again she's asking herself what on earth she's doing and who is this guy, anyway?

* * *

The Parish Women's Association meeting progresses painfully from one item to another. The summer fête. Stalls. A church production of *Lady Windermere's Fan*. Miss Hale will direct. Perhaps even appear? The meeting turns to Emily, and she smiles, nodding, her decision to attend the meeting justified after all, while she contemplates the ripples of gossip that may, at this very moment, be expanding into the greater world where eyebrows will be raised and Tom's head will be left drooping in disappointment.

At the same time there is a screech of car tyres out in the street, and she is relieved to see everybody turn from her to the direction of the sound. And, as it fades, the women, all seated at a long table, look at each other and knowingly raise their eyebrows. The youth of the town, the eyebrows say, would do well to spend more time in its churches than its diners.

The meeting progresses. Time creeps. And when she steps out through the church door it is dark. Across the green, the hall light in her cottage glows, and for a moment she can't remember leaving it on. But then, she reminds herself, she was distracted.

She says goodnight to the ladies of the association, and they all say goodnight to her, adding that they are looking forward to the play. Miss Hale will direct. Perhaps even appear. All is well. The world has returned.

As she steps in the front door she notices nothing unusual. Then she realises, with only slight concern, that it wasn't the hall light that was left on, but the study light. Silly her. But as she switches on the lounge-room lamp and steps into the study to turn the light off, she suddenly understands.

The drawers of her desk have been flung open. Papers and ornaments have been scattered across the top of the desk, the fountain pen knocked from its holder (no modern ballpoint pen for Miss Hale) and the chair is lying sideways in the middle of the room, where it was thrown.

* * *

Grace feels almost sober now. If that's the word. Straight, they call it. But Ted is chuckling, making hoots of excitement every now and then as he counts the money. More than he thought. More than they thought. Old ladies *will* keep money in their houses. And once he's counted the money again and announced that there's more than enough to buy yesterday's guitar, he slips the notes into his pocket.

And it is only then, as they are cruising along through the night, looking for a good place to pull over and take a breath, that he takes out the bundle of papers he's stuffed into his shirt and starts looking at them. At first eagerly, then impatiently. Letters, letters, letters. Useless old letters, with the kind of stamps on them that nobody uses any more.

Grace is concentrating on the road ahead, only half mindful of what Ted is doing. The wind fans his face. One after another, and with increasing impatience, he pulls the letters from their envelopes, ripping an envelope here and a letter there.

'Letters!' he yells out to her. 'Fucking letters!'

He holds one up, switches on the internal light, and tries to read it.

'I have always loved you …' He grabs another and holds that up too, shaking his head as he reads. 'I love you … Emily, Emily, I lurrve you …' he yells, mimicking a popular recording in a sing-song voice, cackling and breaking into laughter.

Suddenly, taking her eyes off the dark road and glancing at Ted and the bundle of letters on his lap, Grace understands. 'They're Miss Hale's letters! Put them back!'

But Ted is cackling and laughing. 'Ooh, Miss Hale's letters!'

He holds another one up to her. 'Useless fucking love letters. All of them. The old bag's love letters. Fucking useless, the lot.'

'Put them back in the envelopes! Leave them!' Grace yells, no longer watching the road, the car beginning to weave from one side to the other.

'Whoa, watch out!'

'Leave them!'

But Ted doesn't hear. Or doesn't want to. Still stoned, or just mad. She straightens the car, then looks back at Ted, the wind fanning his face, and is about to speak again. But before she can do anything, before she has the chance to cut through his manic laughter, before she can get through to him, whoever he is, Ted lifts the letters, half of them removed from their envelopes, half not, and throws them all out the window. He cackles as the flock of white pages and envelopes takes flight. Open-mouthed, Grace watches.

She swings round from the wheel, ignoring the road. 'What have you done? My God, look!'

He is laughing harder. Her outrage is hilarious.

Her foot hits the brake and they come to a loud, screeching stop. A lone car on a deserted country road. She turns, he turns. And they both watch as a white cloud of letters is lifted by the wind and carried swiftly across a farmer's field. They rise, they fall, they scatter. Helpless. The wind has them. Letters, ripped from their envelopes; envelopes bearing the stamp images of dead kings – all float helplessly on the wind, and, within seconds, are blown from view, one by one gradually disappearing into the darkness. As if they never existed.

She glares at him. 'You idiot! You fucking idiot!'

His laughter is dying down.

'She *knew* someone. Miss Hale had a thing with someone famous.'

'Ooh!' He erupts into laughter again. 'Who?'

'I don't know,' she cries, her head falling back on the seat. 'Somebody really famous. I don't know, some … some sort of Shakespeare.'

He is unmoved. 'So?'

She is bolt upright again. '*So?* Would you throw Shakespeare's letters out the window?'

He grins, lets out a cackle, and she nods to herself. Yes, yes, you would, wouldn't you. And straight away, she knows that her Ted days are done, her Ted phase finished. Fun for a time, but the fun just ran out.

She points at his stomach, where something is still concealed under his shirt. 'What's that?'

'Junk!'

'Give it to me!'

'Have it!' And he flings a small book, a diary, Grace notes, or a journal, across the seat. It slaps into her lap. He lets out a snort.

She scans the dark, bare field. Miss Hale's letters are nowhere to be seen. Somebody famous. And all she can picture is the golfer, the famous golfer, in tweed shorts, socks and a cap, sometime long ago. Shakespeare in plus-fours. The letters, apart from the photograph, possibly all she had left. How in heaven's name did she ever get herself into this? Miss Hale may not miss the money, but she will miss the letters. Yes, it was one thing to steal her money and tell yourself she wouldn't miss it. But this is different. And she'd dearly love to scoop the last few hours up, along with the money and letters, and put them back in Miss Hale's drawer. As if nothing had happened. But it has. She looks at Ted with utter contempt. 'You idiot.' And she knows, as she says this, shaking her head in disbelief, that she's talking about herself as much as Ted. 'You *fucking* idiot!'

His grin fades, the cackles subside. She's calling him an idiot. A fucking idiot. And he doesn't like it. His smile slips easily into a sneer, his lip curls. And suddenly she's staring at a stranger. She's on the point of calling him a small-town nobody as well, but holds back.

'*I'm* an idiot? Who's parked in the middle of the road?'

Her foot pounds heavily onto the accelerator and she swings the car round, stirring up the dust, and speeds back into town. The journal on her lap. Ted, the stranger with a sneer on his face, beside her. More than a touch of violence in his eyes that she should have seen coming, but, like a lot of things, didn't. There are no cars about and the trip back to town is fast. And silent.

She doesn't even look at Ted, say goodbye or acknowledge him in any way when she pulls up at the diner in the main street. Just parks, switches the engine off, leaps out into the street, clutching the journal, and walks away without so much as the slightest of backward glances.

'Bitch!' she hears Ted call from the car. 'You'll be back, Miss Marilyn Monroe. You'll be back!'

His cries fade in the deserted street as she strides away. Eyebrows raised, she could almost laugh. Marilyn Monroe, indeed. Yesterday's goddess. Yesterday's insults. Typical Ted, yesterday's man to the last.

* * *

Her steps take her, without any great conscious thought, to Miss Hale's cottage. At first Grace is unsure if it's the right thing to be doing or not. Then she looks down at the journal she is clutching as fiercely as she was when she leapt out of the car, and she knows she must do this. The journal must be returned. At least this much can be put right.

The light in Miss Hale's lounge room is still on. It's not that late, after all. And she debates with herself about whether to approach the cottage or not, in case she is seen by Miss Hale or anybody else. But there is no one else about. The church is shut up. This part of the town is deserted now, apart from the occasional passing car. It won't take long. So, quietly, in the darkness, she walks across the lawn, and, seeing there is no letter box, approaches the house. Music from a gramophone rises to meet her. A song, a singer, a scratchy record. She lifts the mat at the front door and places the journal underneath. It will be safe there until morning, when Miss Hale emerges and sees it. She hasn't opened the journal and she has no desire to. It is not hers. It is Miss Hale's. And she hopes that the return of the diary or the journal, whatever it is, will in some way compensate for the loss of the letters, now strewn in the dark across a farmer's field. Eventually to be rained on, turned to mush and ploughed back into the soil, along with leaves and twigs and whatever else lands on the field, borne in by the wind.

As Grace stands at the door she steals a quick glance in the front window, and there, with her back to Grace, is the seated figure of Miss Hale. Smoke is rising from her fingers, there is a drink on the table beside her. A crackling record plays. A song. The clear voice of the singer coming through the crackle. Miss Hale is in a world of her own. There is no danger of being observed. Words, here and there, become clear: dreaming waves, and delight that is all alone. The record finishes. Miss Hale puts her cigarette down. She lifts the needle, and the song starts again. Smoke rises from her fingers. Miss Hale has not so much withdrawn to her room as from the world. Out of view, the man dressed like a golfer – this Shakespeare with whom Miss Hale had a thing – smiles, no doubt, back at her, as he will always do. And for the first time, Grace is seriously wondering what happened between them. What stopped them? What stood in their way? What could have been so powerful? Miss Hale's past has never seemed so distant and unfathomable.

Grace quietly leaves; the scene is as undisturbed as when she came upon it. Miss Hale is in a world of her own. A time of her own, for there is something untouchable about her at this moment. No ding, no dong of the church clock striking the hour; no car horn; no voice can disturb her. She is, Grace notes with a reassured sigh, safe. Miss Hale is in her world. And as Grace crosses the lawn towards the street for the short walk home, where her father will be concerned that she is not back (but not too concerned, for she is a big girl now), she carries with her the picture of Miss Hale in her chair, smoke rising from her fingers with the crackling music, and the inkling that she too, sooner or later, will sit in such a way, similarly removed from the world, because the world outside won't be hers any more. But, she tells herself with a lighter heart, not just yet. Not for some time. For between now and then there is a whole life to be lived, and if Miss Hale has taught her anything, beyond correct breathing, diction and rhythm, it is just to live, so that when, at last, she sits in that chair, smoke rising from her fingers with the crackling of music, it will be the solace of the *lived* life that she will draw on as much as her cigarette.

* * *

Emily stands looking at the desk, then sinks into the chair. The desk can be cleaned up. That's no great matter. But the drawer has been left open and she can plainly see that the contents have been taken. Odd, earlier in the day she was ready to throw the letters into the sea along with the journal, so that the world would never get its grubby hands on them. But in the end, she couldn't. Now this. The world, indeed, has got its grubby hands on them, but not the grubby hands she imagined.

Has Chance done what she could not bring herself to do? But when she thinks past the sense of intrusion – or is it a sense of violation? – she's asking herself if it was chance, after all. When, for whatever reason, we choose one course of action over another, are we setting wheels within wheels in motion, a whole clockwork mechanism that assumes a life of its own and may look like chance, but which, all the same, can be traced back to its origin with all the logical inevitability of a tragedy? Or a good detective story?

She rises from the chair and begins tidying the desk. She wipes the surface, if only to rid herself of that sense of intrusion, that sense of a complete stranger standing where she is now, deciding what to take and what to leave, before she even thinks about such things as fingerprints. She puts the photographs back in place (her mother, her aunt and uncle, friends, and one of the young Tom just before he left Boston and never came back), returns the ink bottle and the fountain pen to their usual places, sits up the *Concise Oxford Dictionary* and a weighty *Companion to Theatre*, then closes the bookends on them. She shuts the drawer, bare except for a few business cards and pencils. Soon, everything is as it was. Except the letters are gone, and the journal she's held on to for – how long is it now? – twenty-five, twenty-six years?

Too long. Her impulse to tip the lot into the sea was possibly right: right for Tom, so that nobody, no grubby journalist, ambitious young professor or snooping reporter would ever pry into the private world of Tom and Emily; right for Emily, a way of casting off what had to be cast off, the satchel and all it contained removed from her neck like some long-borne albatross, so that she could, at last, be free of it all.

She's walking around the cottage wondering how the thief got in when she comes to a lounge-room window that has been forced open. The lock is broken, the flyscreen pulled back. No other room has been touched: not the bedroom, lounge room or kitchen. The thief came in through this window and knew exactly where to go. Who would know? A workman? Not really. A travelling salesman? No, they never get in the door. One of her girls? And straight away she's remembering Grace, right there, in that lounge-room chair that looks into the study, with that mark on her neck and saying, 'He's a bit of an animal.' And she'd flinched as if having let a bit of animal into the house. And perhaps she had. For when she stands at a certain spot in the lounge room she sees straight away that a trick of the mirror that she's never noticed before catches the desk and the drawer.

Grace. But could she, really? No. For as much as the girl has a touch of the wild about her, Emily also trusts her. Then she remembers that boyfriend of hers, the animal, and she can readily conceive of him doing such a thing. Had Grace told him, after all? Probably. At the same time, the weight of the past — of waiting and watching for the beast to leap and the great event to announce itself — now fallen from her, she's asking herself, what of it? Perhaps it is all for the best. Nothing but some spare change and letters have been taken. And was it chance or do these things have an irresistible, fated logic to them? The constituent parts of the day's events were there all along: Emily, Tom, the letters and the journal (stuffed hastily into a drawer), Grace and the animal. That and so much more: one's whole history, right down to the decision to go to the parish meeting tonight as apart from staying at home just this once. Is everything so finely interwoven that nothing takes place by chance? And did what we call 'chance' step in and do the very thing that she couldn't bring herself to do?

She doesn't need the letters. She has her memories. And nobody can steal them or pry into them. Nobody can get their grubby hands on your memories and turn them into cheap reading, something to while away the time between trains. No, they're safe now: Tom is safe, Emily too. The letters are gone. What of it? 'Chance' has done its work.

When she's closed the window as best she can for the time being, she returns to the lounge room and takes a portable record player from the sideboard, places it on a table next to one of the armchairs, takes the Scotch from the drinks cabinet and pulls a packet of cigarettes from the sideboard drawer. Tom always liked a Scotch, and in those years between the wars when they were visiting each other, both here and there, she'd pour him his Scotch in the afternoon. Just like a wife, greeting her husband at the end of a working day, the height of the Scotch in the glass an indication of how the day had gone. And as she pours the spirit into the glass now, the quantity is commensurate to the nature of the day. Then she takes an old record from the rack, puts it on the turntable, lowers the needle and sits back in the armchair.

The room is filled with the sound of crackling, and then it begins. Smoke rises from her fingers, Scotch warms her veins. The sound is thin, but she likes that. She could easily have – what is it? – a Hi Fi, but she prefers this. For the thin, scratchy record gives her not only the experience of the music but of the times themselves when the music spoke of those emotions, that now extinct order of feeling, that they themselves couldn't speak of. A voice, clear and pure beneath the crackling, sings of dreaming waves and lone delight, and that long-ago parlour comes back to her: that small room, the guests all friends or family, and Tom, eyes darker than anything she had ever seen, a Gioconda smile on his lips. She knew he was hers. That she had him, before she lost him. And they spent the years between the wars trying to regain a lost life that was already lost forever.

* * *

The next morning, one of bright sunshine and early warmth, she sees the hump under the front door mat straight away. And

206

with a mixture of deep relief and trepidation, like someone welcoming back the weight of a responsibility they thought they'd discarded, she retrieves the journal, which is looking a little soiled after spending all night under the door mat. She places it in a cardboard box for such things that she keeps in her bedroom (and where the letters and the journal would have been the previous evening had she not been hurried), and returns the box to the wardrobe.

Grace has been and left it. Who else? Not such a bit of an animal, after all. But one of her girls – *hers*, as they have always been. Drawn back by loyalty. Emily crosses the lawn and turns into the main street. She stops at the diner, which is also a sort of bakery. The Concord Women's Club meets this morning and every month she brings cakes and doughnuts that she buys here. The doughnuts always go first. So she is concentrating on the range of cakes on display when she enters the diner and doesn't notice a small group in the corner, gathered round the jukebox.

But when she looks round from selecting the cakes, she notices them, and sees, sitting at the centre of the group, the young man she observed yesterday with Grace. The animal, she supposes. And who, Emily decides instantly, is beneath Grace. She can almost hear herself warning the girl. Never, dear Grace, *never* marry beneath yourself. I had a friend, a very dear friend, who made a most unfortunate marriage and was almost destroyed by it. Never marry beneath yourself. And observing the scene from the front counter, it is with a certain satisfaction that she notes that Grace is not with him. She watches him for a moment as he displays a guitar to this small group with all the enthusiasm of a child showing off a new toy. An electric guitar. And little that she knows of these things, it looks costly. Beyond this young man's means. He looks up briefly and sees Emily. And with all the authority that comes of being Miss Hale, Emily stares directly back at him and nods. A look that says, I know exactly what happened; don't imagine for a minute I don't, young man. And Ted recoils, instantly looking away like someone blinded by sunlight on an icy puddle. It is an exchange that contains both accusation and guilty admission. And the satisfaction is all Emily's. She has her victory. A bit of an animal, true. But a lesser species of animal: one easily stared down. Beneath her, beneath Grace. Beneath Tom. Beneath them all. One of the low who will always recoil from the scrutiny of their betters. It is enough. The point is made.

From the moment she wiped the top of the desk clean the previous evening, she knew she would not be contacting the police. The thought of the police walking through her house, listing what was stolen – the letters, *private* letters – was almost like delivering them into the grubby hands of the world herself. No, just as the young man is beneath Grace, so too the police are beneath Emily. She could not drag Tom through it, nor could she ever bring suspicion on one of her girls. Or put her through whatever may follow. No, there is no point. She has had her satisfaction.

And it is while she is confirming all of this to herself that a song starts up on the jukebox: the same song Grace has often noted, somebody's favourite. There is a jingle and a jangle, like all the songs now, and yet when this song starts it sounds strange in her ears, but wondrously so: as if it were at least three hundred years old and written by nobody in particular. Blown in on the wind over a wild field. A community creation, if created by anybody at all. If it were a poem, the author would be *Anon.* Some songs are like that, sound as though they have always existed. It sounds wondrously strange in her ears, and she is drawn into it. Words that she only partly hears: a line here, a phrase there. Lines that, because she can't hear them properly, she's not even sure she hasn't made up herself. As though not only were they written by nobody in particular and in no particular time, but were also constantly being written and rewritten: a constantly evolving chorus. And in this song the singer is telling an unnamed listener to lay down his tune, his weary tune. As you might tell a soldier to lay down his sword or a poet to lay down his pen. The drummer to lay down his drum; the bugler, his bugle. The time for such things as battles, poems and reveilles is done. Soldier, drummer and poet alike have given their all and can give no more. Lay down your weary sword, your weary sticks, your weary pen. Lay down, lay down. Lay down and rest ye, weary soul. Lay down ... And she is so drawn into this strange, this haunting, timeless sound that she barely notices when her cakes are handed to her.

The chirpy voice of the young woman behind the counter breaks the spell. The young man guiltily lays down his guitar, placing it in its case. The song continues, but Emily is no longer drawn deep into it. The spell is broken. All the same, it stays with her as she leaves the diner, haunting her, following her down the street like a fog on a wintry night.

* * *

Miss Hale might think of Grace as old for her age, but if she were to tell her at this moment, Grace would answer that today is the first of her grown-up life. The difference between one day and another, although not often, can be that dramatic, and Grace is just discovering this. She knocks on Miss Hale's door. Once, twice. But she's not in. She keeps busy, Miss Hale. Grace stands at the door, a duffle bag on the ground beside her, and looks around for a sign of her teacher. Nothing. She takes out a letter. No stamp, just Miss Hale's name on the envelope. For it is a letter that was always meant to be hand delivered. It is a letter she has given much thought to, for it has been a night of much thought and little sleep. And many imagined drafts: a letter of guilt, confession, apology.

But in the end, she wrote a thank-you letter. The sort one of Miss Hale's girls might write upon leaving school: part play-acting, partly sincere. But mostly true. For she has heard of Miss Hale and her girls, the loyalty of her girls. And she would not like to be remembered as the only one of her girls who ever failed her. So she has written a thank-you letter: not for anything in particular – lessons, advice, conversation – not for any one of these, although she does mention them. No, it is for the experience of having known Miss Hale, an experience, she knows, that will stay with her through the years.

For Grace, over the last few months, and for all the times she's laughed at Miss Hale behind her back, has come to think of her as a kind of cry from one age to another. One that she's only just heard, a realisation that has just crept up on her; and last night in dreams or dreamy half-sleep, Miss Hale tapped her on the shoulder: don't laugh, she said in that soft, proper way of hers, don't laugh, but I could have been you, and you me. You and I, we are very similar after all – the difference between us is merely a matter of timing. And your timing is better than mine. She fixed her with her eyes like an older, a distant sister, and then she was gone, her words a cry from what would have been an incomprehensibly distant world had Miss Hale not come along and made it comprehensible. A stifled cry from another world altogether: a world of parlours and lounge rooms overseen by the stern, framed faces of the dead and the living, the keepers of the script as well as of the faith; those stern faces whose power to sway and to cower is not diminished by death but enhanced by it. What must it have been to grow up with them staring at you? Like having God himself watching your every action and reading your every thought. What must it have been? For there was something inside Miss Hale that they, these keepers of the faith, were all afraid of: some impulse to *live* that was beneath her, beneath them all, something even rough, a bit of an animal, that never got out. Only its cry did. Grace registered, but she didn't hear properly until last night when she watched Miss Hale listening to the old gramophone and a silent cry seemed to rise up from her with the cigarette smoke: for a stage she never stood on, a song she never sang, a love that fled, a life she never lived. Yesterday Grace was too young to take it all in; today she's not. All of it incomprehensible, until Miss Hale came along and made it comprehensible. And so, as much as Emily Hale may think of Grace as old for her age, today feels like the first day of Grace's grown-up life.

The events of the previous night are like a bad dream now; she, another Grace altogether. What on earth was she doing? But it wasn't a dream. It was her. And as she taps her chin with the envelope in the bright summer sun, she's asking herself how old do we have to be before we take responsibility for what we do: ten, twenty, eighty? Ted, she knows, is one of those who never will. And her mother (when was the last time she even heard from her?), Grace is beginning to suspect, another. And this, perhaps, is the difference between yesterday's Grace and today's. And as she drops the letter through the flap in the door for the mail, she's feeling like an Alice who's come back from her summertime adventures and grown back to her normal size. An older and wiser Alice, who's done something beastly and promises not to again, and who has come to say thank you, Miss Hale, for making the incomprehensible comprehensible, and hopes it's not too late.

But perhaps it is. Grace picks up the duffle bag and ambles across the lawn towards the main street, which leads down to the station and the train to Boston. She is sure Miss Hale, like those keepers of the faith who oversaw her every action and knew her every thought, knows everything. But is also sure she would never report Grace. For apart from shrinking at the thought of inviting the police into her house, she would be reporting one of her girls, and that would reflect badly on both of them. No, she corrects herself with a smile, it would be beneath them.

On the way to the station she passes the diner and looks through the window. No Ted. That's good. But in the usual corner where the jukebox sits, three familiar faces sing along to a pop song. I'm a little bit wrong, the song says, you're ... She waves, they wave back. She's knows it's goodbye; they don't. No Ted. That's good. Ted, in the end, was nothing more or less than a small-town nobody. And as much as she knows her Ted phase has just ended, she's also asking herself what on earth she was thinking in starting it. How could she? And with a jolt, she realises that she has just passed a Miss Hale judgement on Ted. That he is beneath her, and always was. What did Miss Hale say once? Never marry beneath yourself: I had a friend once ... No, her Ted phase was always going to end, and end badly, but not because he was beneath her or she above him. No, they were just *they*: two people who found something in common for a short while, but were always from different worlds and different times, for, occasionally, the difference between one decade and another can be that dramatic. No, Ted was all right. A rough nut, but all right. She laughs; at least he looked like a poet. And good arms. The right animal – or the wrong one – at the right time, or the wrong one. As the song on the jukebox sang, it was all a little bit right, and a little bit wrong.

The main street is well behind her now as she crosses onto the Boston-bound platform. Some of the town's young people are gathered there: either going away or seeing someone off or, possibly, just come to see the train. Summer holidays, she smiles: doesn't matter where you are, they're always too long, then suddenly too short. But it's a smile tinged with sadness, for it is, she knows, a big-girl observation. She spoke to her father that morning at breakfast. She was a big girl now, she said. Eighteen. He nodded. And this was a small town. He nodded again. She wanted out. To go back to their home in New York. Back to Washington Square. She could look after herself, she really could. And, to her amazement, her father nodded a third time. He believed her. Perhaps it shows, the difference between one day and another. And so here she is. Boston bound; New York by late afternoon. Why not, her father said. Why not, he'd be back in a few weeks himself. And with that, her small-town phase was over. And Ted with it.

Somewhere out there, beyond the houses, there's an open field strewn with letters and envelopes, at rest on the ground with no wind now to stir them. And with the image of the letters at rest on that bare field, she's remembering the moment the previous night when they were all flung from the car window, took flight and floated out into the breezy air, gradually disappearing into the darkness. And with that the sound of Ted's manic cackle. I love you, I love you, I looooove you, he'd sung. No, not sung. What do you call it, what would her father call it? Crooned. Yes, that's it. But not the sort of crooning that'll ever get you on record. No, just the usual singalong crooning that accompanies any jukebox in any diner. I love, I love you, I looooove you ...

The clang-clang of the locomotive breaks into her thoughts as the train enters the station. She takes a quick look at the rag-tag collection of kids and travellers around her, takes a final glance back towards the town, then steps on, duffle bag slung over her shoulder. Her heart leaps. Boston bound; New York by late afternoon.

Epilogue

There are letters that are lost in the sense that someone put them some place and forgot where, only for them to be discovered a hundred years later and opened once again to a changed world. And there are also letters that are burnt or thrown out with the rubbish, and become lost forever, with no hope of recovery. Emily Hale puts her lost letters in that second category. 'Chance' had stepped in where her will had failed. In the end, it was the right ending.

She can barely remember the drive to Rockport. She has parked the car near the wharf and is now sitting on a bench overlooking the rocks. They are distant, possibly three or four miles away; she's not sure. The view from the bench is not ideal, but good enough. The Dry Salvages. *Les Trois Sauvages.* In the late-afternoon light, though, they hardly look savage. There's no wind. The sea is calm. The water still. The waves lap about the whale hump and those granite teeth surrounding it. She *might* have offered the letters to the sea and the god of the rocks. They *might* now be either floating around the rocks or have drifted out to sea or become entrapped in seaweed.

But it's not so much the letters she's contemplating, as she looks out over the water, as the question of the lives we live and the lives we don't: what comes to pass and what might have come to pass. If your mood had been different on a certain day; if you had not assumed the luxury of time to change this or that in your life and put it in order; if the world had not been so large and Tom *not* gone into that large world, where the wrong somebody emerged from its largeness far away to change everything so that it would never be the same again.

She stayed in a kind of contact with Tom till the end, through his writings and his interviews. Especially the interview in which he talked about the mug's game of writing: a phrase that she'd heard from him long before the world or his young wife did; a phrase carrying with it the confession that the price for what the world calls art and fame was too high, and that he might well have lived another life altogether. That others might be well satisfied with their chosen paths, might not feel that they have wasted their time and messed up their lives for nothing – but not him. And for the last five or ten minutes she has been lost in a world of speculation, contemplating that other life. As if life – his, hers, theirs – were a story with many beginnings and many endings. A constant negotiation. Continually evolving. Or imagined.

The scene is a large house in some university town. A man returns home after a day's work, carrying a briefcase full of essays to be marked, lecture notes and notices about staff meetings and the coming event of a visiting distinguished scholar or writer. And although he has been working all day, he bears the face of a man content with life. Even happy. She pours him a drink as he sinks into his usual armchair, the measure of the drink commensurate to the nature of the day. The children know to leave him alone for the next half-hour or so, then he is theirs. For this man was born to have children, numerous children. About ten of them. Although, in her mind, Emily draws the line well before ten. All the same, she's not exactly sure where. They sit, they talk. At ease with each other; at ease with the world.

And when the familiar routine of the evening meal is done and the children have scattered to various parts of the house or garden (for it is summer, just as it is now), he retires to his study. But instead of marking the essays in his briefcase, he takes a manuscript from his desk drawer. A book of poems. For he writes poetry in his spare time. Has for years. And this manuscript is the result. He opens the folder and looks at the poems, one after another, always correcting them, always writing or rewriting them. Poems with odd characters that have odd names such as Prufrock, Sweeney and Burbank; street lamps that talk; and Boston ladies of a certain age who serve tea with biscuits as brittle as themselves.

They will never be published. He knows that. Not because they are not good enough, for he has no idea of their merit. Whether they're good or not. He's not even sure what that means or if it matters. No, they will never be published because he will never send them to a publisher. These poems are where he goes in his spare time. His retreat. His other world. And he has no intention of losing them *or* that other world. Has Emily read them? Possibly, possibly not. She's not sure about that, sitting on the bench, watching the waves lap about the rocks, while a state away Grace's train completes its journey and she watches the mellow evening light fall across the wonderland of Manhattan.

No, if he were ever to give them up to the arbiters and the gods of the reading public, he would lose those spare hours in which he writes and rewrites them. For they are an endless source of pleasure and amusement and constitute that other world that everybody must have, and which he goes to when time allows, occasionally contemplating what would have happened had he pursued the mug's game of poetry, as he fully intended to as a young man.

And would it have mattered, anyway? A world without Prufrock? A world in which Prufrock and all his co-creations remained locked away in the drawer of the desk of a philosophy lecturer, professor material, who spends more time correcting essays than writing poems; who is content to sink into an armchair at the end of the day, a Scotch glass of varying quantity in his hand, with the sound of numerous children running through the house and the garden? Would it have really mattered, after all?

No T.S. Eliot. No public man. Just Tom. Tom Eliot, a philosophy lecturer who once harboured poetic ambitions, but, like most young men, grew out of it. And Emily – an actress who did tread, for a short while, the stages of Boston and New York, but wearied of it – a different young woman in that Cambridge garden all those years before: the world no less of an annoying place but Tom not held responsible for it, her response to his stammered declaration to her confirmation that they were both of like affection and a like mind. Their meeting ending with a pledge: that he would return. That she would wait, and together they would watch unfold the great event of their lives: the sheer, wondrous ordinariness of it all.

That was the life that never happened. But would it have mattered, after all, if it had? If the man were happy? Not a wreck? And if the Lady were *there*, not withdrawn?

The grey-blue sea is turning orange. The rocks, the Dry Salvages, are ghostly in the twilight: the rocks that the young Tom, sailing these waters in a catboat called *Elsa*, observed time and again. Emily never saw the boat, but he spoke of it often. These rocks, these waters, these headland pines, he took with him, for as much as he may have left these shores, they never left him. And in a way, he never left at all.

Emily shifts on the bench as the song from that morning in the diner returns to her. Not so much a song, as a 'thing'. Written by nobody in particular. Or nobody at all. Blown in on the wind. Not written by anybody in particular, and belonging to no particular time. Lay down, Tom. Lay down your song, your pen, your dreaming waves; your lone delight. The effort of a lifetime took everything. You have given more than you ever dreamt, or knew. Lay down your weary body.

221

Your work is done. No worldly hand can touch you now. No cold doubt. Neither censure nor approval can reach you now in the swirling seaweed and lapping waves against the rocks. Lay down, Tom. Lay down.

Emily stays on the bench as the blue-grey sea turns to orange and black, then she rises and takes the short walk back to her car. Couples, families, children in varying numbers pass around her: the sheer, wondrous ordinariness of it all. And, no doubt, some of them will turn and watch with either curiosity or amusement as she withdraws into her car: the car itself a curiosity. And just to give them all something to think about, when the lead foot of Emily Hale hits the accelerator, her hand comes down on the car horn, emitting a sound that is almost prehistoric, like a cry from one age to another.

Notes for a Novel

This is an abridged version of Steven Carroll's essay 'Notes for a Novel', published two years before *A New England Affair*, in *Meanjin*, vol. 74, issue 2, 2015

It was the question of accent that took up most of the conversation at my first meeting in Cambridge, Massachusetts, with the editor of the *Harvard Review*, Christina Thompson — also a former editor of *Meanjin*.

Did the St Louis-born Eliot come to Harvard in 1908 with a Missouri accent and did he leave it here or lose it here, by accident or design?

It was a question that I also put to the poetry curator of the Lamont Library. And the consensus was that nobody really knows and nobody ever will, since, among other things, there are no recordings of Eliot in his youth. It was generally agreed that the Missouri accent is pretty neutral anyway and it wouldn't be all that difficult to lose. All we can say with any certainty is that, at some point, Eliot acquired *that* voice, the voice that became synonymous with T.S. Eliot. And he never lost it.

But why care? Who would care? A novelist might. I've written two Eliot novels [before *A New England Affair*]: *The Lost Life* and *A World of Other People*. The first revolves around 'Burnt Norton', the second around 'Little Gidding'. And I'm currently researching the third in what I plan will be a quartet of novels, each revolving round one of the *Four Quartets*. And that's what's brought me to Cambridge. Harvard is where Eliot studied – at first indifferently, then very seriously indeed. This is where he wrote 'The Love Song of J. Alfred Prufrock', 'Portrait of a Lady', 'Preludes', 'La Figlia Che Piange' and many more poems that formed the basis for his first collection of poetry, *Prufrock and Other Observations* (1917).

It is commonly agreed among writers and critics that this is the collection that gave birth to modernist poetry, and as much as readers might imagine that these poems are set in either London or Paris, they're set in Cambridge. Or back in St Louis, where Eliot grew up. And, as much as readers might imagine that Eliot was quintessentially English, he was American. He left Boston in 1914, never to live permanently in America again, and became an English citizen in 1928. But, as many contemporaries observed, as much as he tried to be English he never got his Englishness right and remained, essentially, an American: a Massachusetts Yankee in Sloane Square. He always maintained that in its wellsprings his poetry was American. And it's this Eliot, the American Eliot, that I've come to research. Hence the question of his accent upon arriving at Harvard. The novel I've got in mind will not be set in Eliot's youth, but it will hark back to it. For it's in Cambridge that Eliot first fell in love (and, arguably, never fell out of love) and here, to a large extent, that Tom Eliot became T.S. Eliot.

As incidental as it may seem, the nature of Eliot's accent, the accent of Tom Eliot, is one of those details that can help define a character – like someone from a working-class background learning to talk in a cultured voice. It's something that was touched upon in *A World of Other People* – when one of the characters listens to Eliot read his poetry, but soon becomes so absorbed by the question 'How does anyone acquire a voice like *that*?' that he ceases to hear the words and is conscious only of the voice.

Eliot, keenly aware of his Americanness, was, nonetheless, always gravitating towards Europe, especially France and England. His destination, geographically and artistically, was always Europe. And if the Harvard undergraduate gradually left his Missouri accent somewhere in Harvard Yard or out there in the streets of Cambridge (which he often walked alone at night in search of poetic images), it might be interesting for those around him to observe Eliot slipping in and out of the two, all part of the process that eventually produced Mr Eliot. It's a detail that may or may not come into the novel, depending on how it pans out.

Above all, though, for these books to work there has to be a story. In *The Lost Life* the story was a speculative account of Eliot's relationship with Emily Hale – the young woman Eliot fell in love with in Boston before leaving for Oxford in 1914, and whom he left behind, convinced that his feelings had not been reciprocated. He was, it seems, quite wrong – she was just reserved, like him. They met again in 1934 in Chipping Camden, the Cotswolds, and one day in September visited an old estate called Burnt Norton just outside the town. The book imagines a sacred act between the two that takes place in the rose garden of the estate; a sacred act that is profaned by the impulsive act of a young man, who, with his girlfriend, is secretly observing Eliot and Miss Hale from nearby bushes. They are the hidden 'children' the poem refers to, but their laughter (which Eliot hears) is not innocent; rather, it is the jeering laughter of experience.

A World of Other People tells the story of an Australian bomber pilot in the Second World War ('Little Gidding' was completed in 1942). The pilot is the only survivor of a crash-landing the year before – a key aspect of which he has repressed, a common condition at the time known as 'amnesic syndrome in time of war'. He is a deeply damaged man, and it is while he is listening to Eliot read his poem – conscious more of the voice of the poet – that the poem suddenly, and with devastating effect, unlocks the repressed. In this sense the book is about the effect of art on someone. And not necessarily uplifting, for, in this case, the poem contains a terrible secret. In both cases the novels came directly from lines in the poems. And they each had a book in the background: with *The Lost Life* it was two books, Somerset Maugham's *Cakes and Ale* and

L.P. Hartley's *The Go-Between*; with *A World of Other People* it was Graham Greene's *The End of the Affair*. In both cases it took a long time, at least a year, to come up with the stories. And neither book was begun until I had the story. Some books are like that.

The story in the background for this third novel [*A New England Affair*] is Henry James' 'The Aspern Papers'. The novel will be largely set in 1964 and will pick up the story of Eliot, in his last year of life, and Emily Hale, living in Concord just outside Boston. She is known to possess certain letters written by Eliot at a crucial time in their relationship and they become objects of intense interest, to both Eliot (who wants them destroyed) and a young scholar. It's not so much a story yet as a fragment of one, and if these notes have a fragmentary feel it's because they are a kind of thinking out loud.

Standing in the rose garden of Burnt Norton (when researching *The Lost Life*) was, initially, a disappointment: the garden was so small and unprepossessing. Then, on reflection, it seemed appropriate. Likewise number 1, Berkeley Place, Cambridge. This is where Eliot's cousin Eleanor Hinkley lived and where Eliot met Emily Hale for the first time, at a literary party in 1913 in which Eliot played Mr Woodhouse to Hale's Mrs Elton. Eliot fell in love and Emily Hale became his most consistent muse for early poems such as 'La Figlia Che Piange' and, most famously, 'Burnt Norton'. And it's fitting that the house in which they met was not large, even ordinary. It accentuates the emotional intensity that Eliot invested the event and the place with. At the time, Eliot was living a short stroll from the house, in Ash Street. And this is one of the lingering first impressions of this group of family and friends – that they moved in a small circle. The part of Cambridge they moved in is compact. And it's not difficult to imagine the young, ambitious Eliot colliding with first love in an intimate lounge room – and, at the same time, being impatient to assume the world and break free of a predictably comfortable, confining world.

These novels have never presumed to go inside the head of Eliot, for a number of reasons. Most of all, when dealing with a major historical figure from the not-so-distant past, I've always thought it more effective to keep that figure as a presence, even an incidental one. One that can be observed by other characters in the book and who, over time, provide the reader with a composite picture that incorporates all the conflicting views, the contradictions and paradoxes of all living, breathing people. To go inside the head of Eliot would be to provide something of a definitive portrait: tantamount to saying this is what I think he was and this is what made him tick. This is what a biographer does. A novelist ranges more freely and plays, if you like, a dodgier game. In *The Lost Life* and *A World of Other People*, Eliot is many things to the characters whose lives he touches either in fact or in verse. Too hard and fast a definition of a character can deaden that character.

At this stage in my research, I'm not sure how much of a presence Eliot will be – whether he will be in the foreground, the middle ground or the background. All of which involves questions of point of view and structure – through whose eyes do we see him, how can we best move over the years, over events and key incidents and keep things tight? For these are, in many ways, epigrammatic novels. And this one is still at that amorphous stage where many things are possible and nothing has really been decided upon. Not even the plot. That can change. A single image can suddenly take over and shift everything.

A day trip to Rockport and a good walk out to Eastern Point to catch my first glimpse of the Dry Salvages suggests other possibilities, more dramatic and less well-trodden than the plot prompted by 'The Aspern Papers'. For Eliot sailed these waters alone and with friends during his youth, and the rocks (hidden at high tide) have wrecked many a ship. The nearby port of Gloucester is where Kipling set his novel *Captains Courageous*, and Eliot was well aware of the seafaring tales that have grown up around this part of the world. And he did go missing for a day or two during one of his sailing ventures. Perhaps that's where my story lies – in these New England harbours and in the Atlantic that Eliot sailed.

These notes are a kind of thinking out loud, and as much as I might imagine I've got the basis for a story, I mightn't have anything at all. With both previous Eliot novels I had the stories worked out before I started, but it took a long time to arrive at that point. So, after a week of walking around Cambridge, I'm beginning to return to the key images that interested me when I started thinking of the book: the twenty-year-old Eliot walking into the library of the Student Union and discovering, through Arthur Symons' *The Symbolist Movement in Literature*, Jules Laforgue, the poet who gave Eliot his poetic voice and poems the likes of 'Prufrock' and 'Portrait of a Lady'; and a 76-year-old Eliot standing in his office at Faber & Faber watching a surging crowd in Russell Square there to greet the Beatles, and being, for all his high-art assumptions, perfectly aware that he is watching a cultural phenomenon, one that almost leaves him feeling obsolete, yesterday's man. For there are two Eliots in this novel: one the young, ambitious artist intent on shaking things up, and the older Eliot, in his last year, his works done, obsessed with posterity. Perhaps this is where the letters he sent to Emily Hale all those years ago when he was young, and, by Eliot's standards, reckless, come into play. For the Eliot watching that anarchic, surging crowd is intent on controlling everything about his life and legacy, so that the portrait that survives him will be a carefully orchestrated one. But the letters that convey a different Eliot, a reckless, even cruel one, can't be controlled because they are in somebody else's hands: Emily Hale's.

Concord (pronounced to rhyme with 'conquered') is a sedate, postcard town that also happens to be the place where the fighting in the American revolution began. The shot that was heard around the world was fired here. It is also where Emily Hale came to live in retirement after Eliot married his thirty-year-old secretary, Valerie Fletcher (in a secret, surprise wedding that mirrored his first marriage), thereby consigning Hale to a life of rejection and spinsterhood — for that is how she would have seen it. Convinced that Eliot would marry her when Eliot's first wife, Vivienne Haigh-Wood, died, she apparently went a little mad in Concord.

It took a while but not too long (thanks to Christina Thompson and the local library) to track down the house Emily Hale lived in — and we eventually found it, or, at least, two possibilities (the street numbers were changed in 1969, the same year that she died). It's easy to imagine her living her last years in quiet despair in one of those timber cottages opposite a church. Research can be problematic. You can do too much of it and it can deaden a story. For, above all, a novel is a work of the imagination and should not lean on the crutch of research. It's also unpredictable. What seems important at the time turns out to be of no use later when it comes to writing the book — and details that seemed merely incidental at the time can suddenly assume great importance. A sifting process, both conscious and unconscious, sets in and you never really know what the significant aspects of research are until sometime later. The time spent in the Houghton library, going through Eliot's letters to friends and family and their letters to him, the wax seal on Eliot's letters with the imprint of an elephant (he was known by London friends as both 'possum', a nickname given to him by Ezra Pound for his ability to escape trouble by playing dead, and 'elephant' — for his memory), the envelope from 1914, hastily ripped open, containing a letter informing him about the status of a travelling scholarship to Oxford, the small, intricate Christmas cards he sent to his family, may come to nothing at all in informing the book, or may suddenly announce themselves as crucial.

Or it may simply be lingering, general impressions of places such as Cambridge, and that eerie sense of things not really having changed all that much since Eliot's time. For it's not difficult to see the poems in those streets, especially on winter nights, the snow piled up on the sides of roads, and the yellow glow of street lights in the damp night. The streets, the quiet Cambridge houses, seen through the poetry, provide an intimation of the young Eliot who walked them. Just as that sense of the world opening out, becoming wide, along the Gloucester coast, provides an intimation of Eliot at home on the sea in his boat, *Elsa*: both the young Eliot, the explorer circling the Dry Salvages, and the mature Eliot, the old man, who ought still to be an explorer.

I don't imagine starting the book for some time yet, possibly a year or more. Thoughts, impressions, observations, all need to settle. In many ways the best thing that can happen to most research is that it gradually becomes forgotten. What is left is the stuff that is of genuine significance. The stuff that has resonated enough to survive. The stuff that won't go away, that nudges and nags you, and says this is where your book is. In the abstract. For the only way you'll ever know if it was all worthwhile or just a waste of time – the only way you'll ever know if there's a book there at all or if the book is going to work – is by writing it. To an extent it's a leap of faith, to an extent it's calculated gamble: that a story *will* emerge, and that all those aspects of the research that lingered on and resonated most will simply assume their places in the story, as if nothing was ever in doubt and as if writing a novel was the easiest thing in the world. Which it isn't.

POSTSCRIPT

It's interesting to look back on these notes now, if only to remind myself that getting a novel started, getting the ball rolling until it acquires its own momentum, is always difficult. It's also interesting to me because these notes bear very little relation to the novel I eventually wrote.

Fortunately, I dropped the character of the academic prying into Emily Hale's life in the manner of James' character in *The Aspern Papers*: the territory was always too well-trodden to be of any use. In the end James' short story *The Beast in the Jungle* (suggested by Lyndall Gordon's biographies of Eliot) was far more pervasive and important. Also, two novels by Virginia Woolf: *Between the Acts* and *Mrs Dalloway*. The former provided a fascinating glimpse of life in an English village on the cusp of the Second World War; the latter gave me the structure for *A New England Affair*, which is set during one day in Emily Hale's life, but also travels in time back through the years and the key events of her life with Eliot.

Likewise, John Fowles' novels *The Magus* and *The French Lieutenant's Woman* were always lurking.

But many points of interest mentioned in the notes did feed into the finished work. The question of Eliot's accent and his Missouri origins did provide the basis for a number of scenes that looked into Eliot's 'Englishness' – as observed by Emily Hale. The importance of Arthur Symons' *The Symbolist Movement in Literature* also played its part. And the instinct to set much of the novel in and around the port of Gloucester (where the Eliot family summer house is – and which I was lucky to see and be given a tour of) was correct. Especially the impulse to put The Dry Salvages themselves front and centre in the book.

I have taken small liberties with historical details: Bob Russell's 'You Came a Long Way From St Louis', for example, was recorded in 1947, well after the scene set in 1939 – but the metaphor reflecting on unfinished journeys fitted neatly into the dialogue at that chapter.

The book is now done and like all done books gives every impression that it could not have turned out any other way. These notes, for me, at least, are sobering in that they remind me that nothing was set in concrete, that there were many false scenarios explored and blind alleys blundered down before I finally finished with a story; that there was much trial and error in the planning and that novels do tend to be organic, evolving as they go.

Acknowledgments

Many thanks to the following.

To Christina Thompson, editor of *Harvard Review*, for all her help, especially in finding Emily Hale's cottage in Concord; and Fiona Atkinson for showing me around the Eliot summer house at Eastern Point, Gloucester.

Shona Martyn, Catherine Milne and Belinda Yuille at HarperCollins, my editor Amanda O'Connell, and my agent Sonia Land and all the gang at Sheil Land.

I would also like to acknowledge Lyndall Gordon's biographies of Eliot, *Eliot's Early Years* and *Eliot's New Life*, especially her imaginative and astute use of the short fiction of Henry James.

I would also like to acknowledge Virginia Woolf's novels *Between the Acts* and *Mrs Dalloway*; and John Fowles' novels *The Magus* and *The French Lieutenant's Woman*.

I am indebted to the works of T.S. Eliot, whose poems I have admired since high school.

Finally, special thanks to my partner Fiona Capp, for her constant support, suggestions and advice, not just in the writing of this novel but all of them. And to Leo – the lion-hearted boy.

THE LOST LIFE

by Steven Carroll

England, September 1934. Two young lovers, Catherine and Daniel, have trespassed into the rose garden of Burnt Norton, an abandoned house in the English countryside. Hearing the sound of footsteps, they hide, and then witness the poet T.S. (Tom) Eliot and his close friend Emily enter the garden and bury a mysterious tin in the earth.

Tom and Emily knew each other in America in their youth; now in their forties, they have come together again. In the enclosed world of an English village one autumn, their story becomes entwined with that of Catherine and Daniel, who are certain in their newfound love and full of possibility.

From one of Australia's finest writers, this is a moving, lyrical novel about poetry and inspiration, the incandescence of first love and the yearning for a life that may never be lived.

Shortlisted for the Barbara Jefferis Award 2010
Shortlisted for the ALS Gold Medal 2010

A WORLD OF OTHER PEOPLE

by Steven Carroll

London, 1941, and the threat of daily bombings hangs heavily in the air. Jim, a young Australian pilot in Bomber Command, has suffered an unbearable loss when he meets Iris, a forthright young woman trying to find her voice as a writer. *A World of Other People* traces their love affair, haunted by secrets and malign coincidence, as they struggle to imagine a future together free of society's thin-lipped disapproval.

The poet T.S. Eliot, with whom Iris shares fire-watching duties during the Blitz, unwittingly seals their fate with one of the poems from his acclaimed *Four Quartets*.

Cinematic, intense and unflinching, *A World of Other People* is a supremely life-affirming evocation of love in war-time, when every decision, and every day, matters.

Shortlisted for the South Australian Premier's Award 2014
Joint winner of the Prime Minister's Literary Award for
Fiction 2014

FOREVER YOUNG

by Steven Carroll

In the tumultuous period of change and uncertainty that was
Australia in 1977, Whitlam is about to lose the federal election
and things will never be the same again. The times they are
a'changing: radicals have become conservatives, idealism
is giving way to realism, relationships are falling apart, and
Michael is finally coming to accept that he will never be a rock
and roll musician.

A subtle and graceful exploration of the passage of time and
our yearning for the seeming simplicities of the past, *Forever
Young* is a powerfully moving work — clear, beautiful, affecting
— by one of our greatest authors.

Shortlisted for the Victorian Premier's Literary Award 2016
Shortlisted for the Prime Minister's Literary Award 2016